Tough Choices
for Roxie

Best Friends

#9

Tough Choices
for Roxie

Hilda Stahl

CROSSWAY BOOKS • WHEATON, ILLINOIS
A DIVISION OF GOOD NEWS PUBLISHERS

*To Lynetta Chambliss
with love
Thanks for our time together
sharing how things are
and how things can be through Christ*

Tough Choices for Roxie

Copyright © 1993 by Word Spinners, Inc.

Published by Crossway Books, a division of
Good News Publishers, 1300 Crescent Street, Wheaton, Illinois 60187.

Cover illustration: Paul Casale

Art Direction/Design: Mark Schramm

First printing, 1993

Printed in the United States of America

Library of Congress Cataloging-in-Publication Data
Stahl, Hilda.
    Tough choices for Roxie / Hilda Stahl.
       p.   cm. — (Best Friends ; #9)
    Summary: Competition over boys and a difficult new student threaten to break up the Best Friends, a group of girls who play, pray, and work together.
    ISBN 0-89107-711-1
    [1. Friendship—Fiction. 2. Christian life—Fiction.] I. Title.
    II. Series: Stahl, Hilda. Best Friends ; #9.
PZ7.S78244Pu   1993
[Fic]—dc20   92-37055

04		03		02		01		00		99		98		97		96
16	15	14	13	12	11	10	9	8	7	6	5	4	3	2

Contents

1

The Ugly Pig

With butterflies fluttering wildly in her stomach, Roxie Shoulders stood on one foot, then the other as she waited for the Best Friends to get to school for Parents' Day. It was already a minute after 7! Chelsea McCrea, Hannah Shigwam, and Kathy Aber had agreed to meet her as close to seven o'clock as possible in the front hall of Middle Lake Middle School where they were all in sixth grade. Finally she spotted Chelsea's bright red hair, Hannah's shiny black hair, and Kathy's blonde curls in the middle of a mob of parents and kids pushing through the wide glass doors at the front of the school. Cool October air rushed in with them. The three girls eased their way out of the crowd and hurried over to Roxie.

"I thought you'd never get here!" Roxie cried. Her wooden carvings of baby animals were on display in the main case in the hall. It had even been

7

advertised as one of the highlights of Parents' Day. Roxie groaned just thinking about all the posters taped in store windows and bulletin boards or taken home by students. It made her feel like *she* was on display. The Best Friends had promised to stand with her at the display case. She just didn't have the courage to be there alone. What if somebody said her wood carvings were ugly and amateurish and didn't deserve to be in such a prominent place?

Chelsea frowned slightly as she tucked her yellow blouse tighter into the jeans she'd saved forever to buy. "I can't understand why you're so nervous. One of the photographs I took is hanging on the wall right over there, and I'm not nervous." She wrinkled her freckled nose and rubbed her freckled cheek. "Well, not very nervous anyway."

"I sure understand!" Shivering, Hannah pushed the sleeves of her blue sweater almost to her elbows. "I didn't even get my painting ready to hang because I got so scared thinking people would make fun of it and of me since I'm Ottawa Indian."

Her hazel eyes sparkling, Kathy leaned closer to the Best Friends and whispered, "Did any of you see Ty?"

Roxie jabbed Kathy. "How can you even ask about him when I'm feeling so scared?"

Kathy flushed. "Sorry." She glanced around, then gasped. "There he is! Right over there, by that black family."

Roxie grabbed Kathy's arm and pulled. "Forget Ty for now. I've got to get over to my display."

"I never saw that family before," Hannah said. "I should go say hi to them so they don't feel left out." She knew all about feeling left out, and she'd lived all her life in Middle Lake, Michigan.

"Forget about them or about anybody else! You all promised to help me tonight!" Roxie led the Best Friends to the glass case. A family blocked the view of the carvings. A little girl pointed at the carvings and laughed.

"It's funny, Mommie! Look at the piggy."

Roxie froze. Piggy? What had she carved that could possibly look like a pig? Roxie peered around the family at her carvings inside the glass showcase. Her blood froze in her veins. On the glass shelf beside her delicately carved wooden baby animals stood a wooden pig made by someone who didn't know a thing about wood or about carving. And it was painted bright purple, with a black snout and hooves!

Laughing, the family walked away.

Trembling, Roxie pointed at the pig. "Look! Would you just look at that!"

Chelsea peered closer at the ugly pig. "Why'd you put the pig in with your good work?"

"I didn't!" Roxie could barely get the words out around the giant lump in her throat. Her red sweater and new jeans suddenly felt too hot. Her scalp prickled under her short dark hair.

"I'm surprised Mrs. Evans let you put it in there." Kathy turned away from the case and looked around for Ty.

"It's not like the rest of your work," Hannah said.

"Because it's not my work! But it's right there on my shelf with my name, and everyone will think I did it! This is too awful!" Roxie wanted to jerk open the display case and destroy the hideous pig, but the case was locked. Only Mrs. Evans, the principal, had the key.

Just then the African American family the Best Friends had seen earlier stopped at the display case and looked at the carvings.

"I could do better work than that," the oldest girl said with a toss of her mass of black hair.

The woman patted the girl's arm. "Now, Stacia. You don't know a thing about carving."

"I know. But I could still do better work than . . ." Stacia leaned close to the glass to read the tag. ". . . than Roxann Shoulders. She must have no talent—or taste—or she wouldn't have put that horrible purple pig on display."

Roxie stepped right up to Stacia. "I am Roxann Shoulders, and I did not carve that pig!" Roxie wanted to yank the girl's long frizzy hair, but she knew she shouldn't. She was learning to be like

Jesus. He sure wouldn't pull Stacia's hair, no matter how mean she was.

Her black eyes wide, Stacia backed away from Roxie. "You don't have to yell at me. I didn't do anything to you."

The woman tugged on Stacia's arm. "We don't want to cause trouble. Let's look around at the rest of the things." She led Stacia away with the man and the three little girls.

Hannah watched the family walk away, then turned back to the Best Friends. "I wonder who they are? Have you girls seen them before?"

"Who even cares!" Roxie cried. "I'm going to find Mrs. Evans and have her take that pig out of there *now*."

"I'm going to find Ty." Kathy caught Chelsea's arm. "Come with me, will you?"

Tears burned Roxie's eyes. "I think my problem is more important than Ty Wilton, Kathleen Aber!"

Kathy flushed. "Shhh! Not so loud. What if he hears you?"

Hannah nodded at Roxie. "It really is more important. Come on—maybe Mrs. Evans is in her office."

"Or in the gym," Chelsea said. "The gymnastics class is putting on a demonstration in a while." Her little brother Mike had especially wanted to watch that. Someday he wanted to be in the Olympics; gymnastics was his life.

Roxie chewed on her bottom lip. She couldn't look at the horrid purple pig or she'd throw up. "Maybe we should split up to look for her. Whoever finds her can tell her about the pig so she'll unlock the case and take it out."

Chelsea lifted her freckled arm and looked at her watch. "We'll meet back at the display case in ten minutes. It is now 7:10. Synchronize your watches, girls." She giggled. "That was fun to say. Just like in a spy movie."

"This is not a game," Roxie snapped. She darted a look around for Mrs. Evans. The crowded hall was full of parents and children. The aromas of popcorn and coffee covered the smells of perfume and body odor.

Roxie inched her way around people and looked in the gym. Several people sat on the bleachers, and a few kids stood near the floor mat. Mrs. Evans wasn't in there. Abruptly Roxie turned and bumped into Stacia.

"Watch where you're going, will you?" Stacia snapped.

"Sorry." Roxie forced out the word through the angry words filling her mouth. She ducked around several people and headed for the library. She saw Ty Wilton talking to Alyssa Carroll, the head cheerleader. "Kathy won't like that," Roxie muttered as she rushed down the hall toward the stairs to the second floor. The middle school was a three-story brick building. The second floor was for sixth grade; the other two floors were for seventh and eighth graders. They all took turns sharing the gym, the library, the band room, and the cafeteria.

Finally Roxie found Mrs. Evans in the sixth grade science room. She was talking to two women. Mrs. Evans was wearing a black suit with a red blouse that matched her lipstick and earrings. Her short dark hair curled prettily around her oval face. Mrs. Evans talked and laughed as if nothing at all were wrong.

Her nerves tight, Roxie stood nearby. It seemed to take forever for the women to walk away. "Mrs. Evans," Roxie said breathlessly, "I need your help!"

"What's wrong, Roxie?"

"I need you to unlock the display case and take out the purple pig you put in it."

Mrs. Evans frowned. "Purple pig? What purple pig?"

Roxie quickly told her about the pig that was sitting on the same shelf as her carvings.

Mrs. Evans shook her head. "But I don't know a thing about the pig. I didn't put it there!"

"Then who did?"

"I have no idea. I have the only key."

"Where is it?"

"In a drawer in my office."

"Please, can you get it and take the pig off my shelf?"

"Of course." Mrs. Evans hurried toward the stairs, her high-heeled shoes clicking loudly on the tile floor.

Roxie kept as close to Mrs. Evans as she could all the way to the office.

Mrs. Evans opened her drawer, then frowned. "That's strange. I left the key right here." She opened the other drawers in her desk. "I'll ask Mr. Ekland if he took it."

Roxie's heart sank. Just how long would it take to find the superintendent? All this time people would look at the purple pig and think she'd carved and painted it! "Maybe somebody took the key so they could play that terrible joke on me," Roxie said just above a whisper.

"Oh, I just remembered! Miss Norville asked to use the key. She had a piece of art one of her students brought in that she wanted the parents to see. Maybe it was the pig."

"Miss Norville wouldn't want anyone to see this pig!"

"We'll find Miss Norville and get the key from her." Mrs. Evans hurried out of her office, firmly closing the door behind her.

"I'll wait beside the display case," Roxie said. It had already been longer than the ten minutes the Best Friends had agreed on. She saw them waiting for her, and she smiled. It was great to have friends!

She'd gone a long time without any, and now she had three of the very best.

Kathy frowned. "What took you so long?"

Hannah giggled. "We came up with a great idea, Roxie."

Roxie ignored Kathy and turned to Hannah. "What?"

"We stood right in front of the case so nobody could see the pig." Hannah looked proud of herself.

"We did let Kesha look though," Chelsea said. "She wondered what we were hiding, so we showed her. She said she thinks she knows who made the pig."

"Who?" Roxie cried.

"She wouldn't say, in case she was wrong."

Kathy jabbed Chelsea in the arm. "I don't think Kesha knew. I think she just said that to get more attention."

"She's not like that anymore," Chelsea said. She knew Kathy was thinking about when they'd first met Kesha and she'd done whatever she could to attract attention. Now that she lived with a woman who loved her, she didn't need to act that way anymore.

Roxie pushed between Chelsea and Hannah so she could look at the ugly purple pig once again. It was still there. She'd hoped it was a terrible nightmare. It was about three inches high and five inches long. Her carvings were smaller and very delicate. "Why would anyone put that pig with my stuff?"

Just then Mrs. Evans hurried up, the key in her hand. She clicked her tongue when she saw the pig. "Miss Norville said she put something on the bottom shelf. But she didn't know anything about the pig."

Roxie locked her icy fingers together. "So who put it in there?" Who would want to make others laugh at her work?

Hannah held her hand out to Mrs. Evans. "Could I look at the pig?" Hannah loved solving mysteries, and this sure felt like a mystery to her.

Mrs. Evans gave the pig to her. "I can't imagine how this happened. I'm sorry, Roxie. Put it in the office for me when you're finished with it, please. I have to get to the gym." She walked away without a backward glance.

Roxie pressed close to Hannah and studied the pig too. Someone had used a saw to cut the pig out of a thick pine board. The snout and eyes had been gouged out with a knife. Whoever had done it knew nothing about carving.

"Why would anyone put this with my things?" Roxie whispered.

Chelsea and Kathy shrugged.

Hannah took a deep breath. "Somebody wanted to make you look foolish tonight. Do you have any enemies, Roxie?"

She darted a look around. Did she have an enemy she knew nothing about? She shivered.

2

Parents' Day

Roxie dropped the purple pig on Mrs. Evans's desk, then brushed her hands off as if she were trying to get rid of even the feel of it. Her head high, she walked back to the hall and to the Best Friends. The smell of popcorn was stronger and the voices of the visitors louder.

"Now we can have fun!" Kathy stood on tiptoe and looked all around. "Let's find Ty so we can see what he's doing."

Roxie wrinkled her nose. Ty wasn't her favorite person. Sometimes she didn't even like him, because he acted like a snob. "He was in the library talking with Alyssa Carroll a while ago," Roxie said.

Kathy's face fell. "I heard she likes him. Did he act like he was glad to be with her?"

Roxie shrugged. "I don't know. I was too busy thinking about the pig to notice."

"Ty's not even a born-again Christian, Kathy,"

Hannah said softly. "You don't want to go with him."

"I know." Kathy pressed her hands to her heart. "But he's sooo nice and sooo cute!"

Hannah bit her lip as she looked at Chelsea and Roxie, then back at Kathy. "We all agreed last week at our Best Friends Club meeting that none of us would go with unsaved boys."

Kathy frowned, then waved her hand as if to brush away Hannah's words. "That was before Ty started talking to me and writing me notes."

"But you agreed, so it still counts."

"That's right," Chelsea and Roxie said.

Kathy chewed her bottom lip, then sighed a loud, long sigh. "I won't go with him—actually *go* with him. But that doesn't mean I have to stay away from him. I can talk to him and even eat lunch with him. I can even answer his notes."

Hannah frowned. "But then you might fall in love with him and go out with him even though you promised not to."

Kathy narrowed her eyes. "I don't know why you're getting so excited about this, Hannah. It's not as if I'll actually date him. You know I can't really date until I'm sixteen."

"I know. But spending time with him now could lead to dating him later."

"Oh, I give up!" Kathy lifted her hands, then let them fall to her sides.

Chelsea looked at her watch, then at the line of people outside the gym door. "It's time for the gymnastics demonstration. Let's go watch."

Hannah nudged Chelsea and whispered, "Look! That black family's looking at the photograph you took."

"At least that girl Stacia can't laugh at anything about your picture," Roxie said.

Just then the little girl standing nearest to Stacia, dressed in yellow, caught her dad's hand and tugged. "Daddy, let's go to the gym now. It's time for the kids to do gymnastics. I want to learn how someday."

"Go get in line, Ariel," her dad said with a laugh. "We'll be right there."

Hannah smiled. "Now's our chance to talk to them. Let's get in line with them."

Roxie took a step back. "No way! You go ahead if you want, Hannah. I sure don't care who they are. I don't like that girl Stacia."

"You don't even know her," Kathy said impatiently. "How do you know you don't like her? She looks nice to me. Let's go talk to them."

"There's Ty," Roxie said, hiding a grin.

"Where? Where?" Kathy darted a look around.

"By the front doors."

"I want to talk to him. Come with me, will you, girls?"

Roxie grinned. "He's not really there, Kathy. I

just said that to show Chel and Hannah you don't care if we meet the new family or not."

"That's not fair at all!" Kathy crossed her arms and scowled at Roxie.

"Don't fight," Hannah said softly. "We're here to have fun."

Chelsea took a step toward the gym, then said over her shoulder, "We don't have to stay together if we don't want. I'm going to the demonstration. Anybody want to come?"

"I do." Hannah joined Chelsea.

Kathy looked around again. "Well, maybe Ty's in the gym. Sure, I'll go with you."

Roxie shrugged. "Me too." She was glad to see there were several people in line behind the African American family. Hannah would have to find another opportunity to get acquainted with them. Roxie didn't like feeling smug, but sometimes it was hard to have the high standards expected of her because she'd accepted Jesus as her Savior. The others had been Christians longer than she had, so sometimes she wasn't as perfect as they were.

Just as the Best Friends reached the door of the gym Heather Robbins, an eight-year-old girl Roxie baby-sat regularly, ran down the hall, sobbing hard.

Roxie quickly told the Best Friends to go into the gym without her, then hurried over to Heather. She wore a blue dress that she usually saved for church, blue ruffled socks, and black dress shoes.

Roxie stopped her and knelt before her. "Heather, what's wrong?"

"Somebody stole my beautiful pig!" Heather said between sobs. Her bright blue eyes flooded over with fresh tears.

Roxie patted Heather's back to comfort her. "I'm sorry—sooo sorry."

"I made it myself, Roxie!"

Roxie wiped Heather's tears away the best she could with her fingers. "Try to stop crying and tell me what happened. I'll help you however I can."

Heather brushed her dark hair back and took a deep shuddering breath. "I wanted to have a carving on display just like you."

Roxie's eyes widened. Pig? Was it possible?

"So Dad helped me saw a pig out of some wood he had. I made the nose and the eyes, then painted it the best I could. I wanted it to be beautiful! I used my favorite color—purple, with a black nose and feet. I even put it on the shelf with your animals. Now it's gone!"

Roxie didn't know what to say for a long time. She'd thought she'd had an enemy. Instead, she had a special friend who wanted to copy her. Tears blurred her eyes, and she blinked them quickly away. "I know where your pig is."

Heather's face lit up. "You do?"

Roxie nodded. "I thought somebody put the

pig with my things to be mean to me. I didn't know you'd done it."

"I did. Miss Norville unlocked the case to put something else in, and I put the pig in when she wasn't looking." Heather sniffed hard. "Where is my pig?"

"In Mrs. Evans's office. But it's not locked. I can get it."

"Did you take it off your shelf?"

Roxie flushed. "Yes."

"I thought somebody mean had stolen my pig."

Roxie hung her head. Sometimes she was mean when she didn't intend to be. She squeezed Heather's hand. "Let's get your pig."

A few minutes later Heather hugged the ugly purple pig close to her as if it were the most wonderful possession in the world. "Thanks for getting it back for me, Roxie. Now can we put it on display with your carvings?"

Roxie shook her head. "I don't have a key."

"Can you get one?"

Roxie frantically searched for the right words. She didn't want to hurt Heather, but she also didn't want the pig sitting beside her animals. She remembered the Scripture that said if anyone lacks wisdom, she should pray for it, and God would give it to her. She prayed silently right then. "Heather, this is a middle school, and the things on display are done by middle school students. You're in elementary school. Your work belongs there."

"Oh. I didn't know that. Well, okay, I'll take my pig to school tomorrow so Mrs. Cramer can put it on display."

"The kids will probably like it a lot." Roxie knew someone might also tease Heather, and she wanted to prepare her for it. "You know, kids used to make fun of my carvings." Roxie remembered the pain she'd felt because of that. Both her grandpa and her mom carved and were well-known for their work. That had made it even harder for her to show anyone what she'd done. "Sometimes they'd laugh at my work."

"What did you do?"

"Cried. But then I did something I shouldn't have."

"What?"

"I wouldn't carve anything for a long time. Then when I did, I hid it away where nobody could see it." Roxie brushed Heather's hair back from her round face. "But I don't want you to do that. Even if kids laugh at your work or make fun of it, you keep doing it and you keep showing it. You'll get better and better."

"Just like you?"

Roxie nodded. "But I'm still not as good as my grandpa was before he died or as my mom is now."

"Does that make you feel bad?"

"A little. But I know if I keep practicing, I'll get really good—as good as I can be."

Heather smiled up at Roxie. "I want to be as good as you, Roxie."

Just then Roy Marks, the boy who liked Kathy, stopped beside Roxie. He was tall and thin with short, dark hair and eyes as blue as a summer sky. "I see you took the ugly pig out of the case."

Roxie flushed as she frantically tried to think of what to do and say.

Heather burst into tears. "It's not an ugly pig! It's beautiful!"

Roxie scowled at Roy. "It's Heather's pig."

"Oh. Sorry." Roy bent down to Heather. "Is that your first piece of art?"

She barely nodded, but her tears stopped.

"I'm sorry I called it ugly."

"That's okay. Roxie said some people would make fun of it."

"I won't do it again." Roy smiled, flashing even, white teeth. "Someday you might be as good as Roxie."

"Or better," Roxie said, smiling at Roy. She hadn't realized he could be so nice. Until just a few weeks ago he'd spent all his time teasing her and Kathy, especially Kathy.

"I'm taking my pig to my mom so she can put it in her purse before anyone else laughs at it." Heather ran up the hall toward the cafeteria where they were serving punch, cookies, coffee, and pop-corn.

Roy laughed and shook his head. "I made a huge mistake, didn't I?"

"Yeah, but you got out of it. Thanks for being nice to her."

Roy shrugged. He glanced around. "Know where Kathy is?"

"In the gym."

"I guess I'll go find her." He walked a few steps away, then stopped and looked over his shoulder. "Want to come?"

"Sure." Roxie fell into step beside him. Her arm brushed his, and a tiny tingle ran down her spine. She looked at him, then quickly away.

3

Stacia

Trembling, Stacia King followed Mom, Dad, Candace, Ariel, and Tiffany into the back door of Grandma and Grandpa Smith's house. They'd moved to The Ravines, a subdivision in Middle Lake, last summer. Their house usually smelled like fresh paint. Tonight it smelled like brownies. Grandma loved brownies. Stacia stopped in the large kitchen behind Dad. No matter how good it smelled or how nice it was to visit, tonight Stacia felt tension crackle around her. Something wasn't right. She shivered even though it was warm. Why weren't they hurrying home on a school night? Something was up. But what? Somehow she knew it had to do with her. Ever since she'd been chased home from school by a gang of boys for the third time Mom had been acting funny.

Mom hugged Grandma and Grandpa, gave the three little girls a plate of brownies, then sent them to the living room to watch TV. Mom never let them eat sweets at night, or watch TV past nine o'clock either, but tonight she had!

Stacia started to follow the little girls. She always had to go with them while Mom and Dad talked, even though she was already twelve years old. Tonight, however, she was happy to get away from the tension.

"Stacia, we need to talk to you." Mom sounded funny—as if she were going to cry or something.

Her stomach balled into a tight knot, Stacia stopped near the big white refrigerator and looked questioningly at Mom.

Dad curled his hand around Stacia's arm as if he couldn't bear to part with her. That made Stacia feel stranger still.

Grandma and Grandpa sat at their usual places at the square kitchen table. Grandpa's hair was almost white, and he wore faded jeans and a blue plaid flannel shirt. Grandma had white streaks at her temple, and she wore black pants and a warm red sweater. They were both drinking tea. The blue-and-white curtains covered the row of windows behind the table. A huge green leafy plant with bright red flowers hung in the corner beside the windows. Stacia sat at the corner of the table between Mom and Dad. Mom filled cups with tea for herself and Dad and poured a glass of milk for Stacia.

Shivering, Stacia looked at her parents and grandparents. They looked very solemn. Grandpa always looked solemn, but Grandma was usually smiling and talking. Stacia wanted to ask what was wrong, but suddenly her mouth was too dry.

Dad took a deep breath and ran his hand over his tight curls. "Stacia, we've decided to have you go to the middle school here in Middle Lake."

Stacia smiled. Why, that was good news—not bad like she'd expected! "You mean I don't have to go back to Braselton Middle School?" She'd hated school there, but she hadn't said anything to Mom and Dad because she didn't want to make them feel bad.

Mom nodded, her eyes shiny with unshed tears. "We didn't want you walking to and from that school any longer."

"Good." Stacia sighed in relief. She hadn't told Mom how frightened she was every day when she walked to and from school and even while she was in school. She hadn't said anything about how bad the drugs and weapons were in that school either. Mom and Dad couldn't do anything about the drugs or the guns and knives. Other parents had tried, but they'd failed.

Mom and Dad exchanged looks. Stacia's heart sank again. There was more.

Mom took Stacia's hand. "In order for you to

go to the middle school here you'll have to stay with Grandma and Grandpa."

"Stay?" Stacia whispered.

"We'll love having you," Grandma said cheerfully. Grandpa didn't say anything. He didn't even smile.

Stacia's head whirled. Stay with Grandma and Grandpa? Stay after school until Mom or Dad got home from work and picked her up? Is that what they meant? It had to be. They couldn't mean she'd sleep here and eat here all the time from now on. They just couldn't!

"Of course you'll come home for the weekends," Dad said quickly. "We couldn't get along without you if we didn't have you with us some of the time."

Stacia gasped. "Do you mean I have to move in with them?"

"Don't force the child to do anything she doesn't want to do," Grandpa snapped.

Mom jumped to her feet. "Papa, you know she can't stay home and continue going to that school! It's not safe! And we can't afford to send her to a private school."

"Bethany," Dad said gently as he patted Mom's arm, "don't get upset."

Mom turned on Dad. "If you made more money, Nathan, we could afford to buy a house in a different section of town. Then we wouldn't have to worry about Stacia getting killed or molested on her way to and from school!"

Stacia caught Mom's hand. "Don't get mad, Momma. I can take care of myself if I stay home. Honest."

Mom squeezed Stacia's hand, then turned to Dad. "I'm sorry, Nathan. I'm just upset. I know you're doing all you can to get a better paying job."

Grandpa cleared his throat as if he were going to disagree, but he didn't say anything.

Dad slapped a paper down on the table. He looked at Stacia, then stared down at the paper. "In order for you to go to school here we have to give Grandma and Grandpa Smith custody of you. You'll come home on weekends unless it snows so much that we can't pick you up."

Trembling, Stacia shook her head. "No . . . I don't want to stay."

Mom's lips quivered. "You must!"

Stacia gasped. How could they just give her away? Didn't they want her anymore? Suddenly it was very clear to her. They had the three little girls. They didn't need her. They didn't want her. With a whimper Stacia leaned back against the chair.

"Stacia, don't make it hard on your momma," Grandma said sharply. "Be a big girl about this!"

Mom wiped her eyes and sat back down. "It's all right, Mom."

"It's not all right for her to talk back to you," Grandpa said with a scowl.

Mom licked her lips, took a deep breath, and turned to Stacia. "We have your clothes in the trunk of the car. You'll start attending Middle Lake Middle School in the morning. It's all arranged. That's why we went to the Parents' Night there tonight. You'll catch the bus at the street just outside The Ravines. All the kids wait there."

Grandma cleared her throat. "You'll sleep in the spare room. I took out my sewing machine and emptied the dresser so you can use it."

"You'll have rules to follow." Grandpa looked very stern. "And if you break them, you'll be punished. Stay out of your Uncle Anthony's room. Now get your things out of the car and get off to bed. It's late."

Stacia looked helplessly at Mom and Dad. She wasn't used to Grandpa giving her orders.

"Do as your grandpa says," Dad said, sounding very tired as he handed her the car keys.

Slowly Stacia walked outdoors. The night air was crisp and cold. Two days ago it had even snowed. Dad had said if it snowed too much they couldn't get her even on the weekends. Stacia leaned weakly against the car. A dog barked, and a car drove past. Finally she opened the trunk, awkwardly lifted out the suitcase and a plastic bag with the stuffed animals she kept on her bed, then closed the trunk with a snap. When had they packed her things? Tears burned her eyes. Why hadn't Mom and Dad discussed their plans with her? Didn't they think it mattered to her? Maybe she just wasn't important enough to them.

Slowly she walked to the front door. The stairs were nearby. She didn't want to walk through the kitchen where Mom and Dad could see her. Her sisters jumped up and ran to her.

"How come you got your suitcase?" Ariel asked.

"What's in the bag?" Candace tried to look inside.

Tiffany stuck her bottom lip out in a pout. "It's not fair that you get to stay the night and we don't."

"Get away from me and leave me alone!" Stacia jerked the bag out of Candace's reach, then rushed upstairs, the suitcase bumping against her leg.

Stacia stood in the doorway of the spare room, clicked on the light, and looked at the ugly plaid bedspread and curtains. The house was big and beautiful, but Grandma sure didn't know how to decorate. A pile of boxes full of things Grandma wanted to keep stood in one corner. Stacia glared at the boxes. When she was little and Grandma lived in a different house, Stacia liked to see the things Grandma stored away. Now they didn't interest her at all.

Whimpering, Stacia plopped the suitcase at the foot of the bed and tossed the plastic bag of stuffed animals into a corner near a round wicker wastebasket. She clicked on the bathroom light. It would be strange to have a bathroom all to herself. At home she'd had to fight for it, and when she finally got it, she'd have to hurry so someone else could use it.

She wrinkled her nose at the ugly green rug in front of the stool and the ugly green cover on the stool lid. The green clashed with the green leaves in the wallpaper.

Sighing, Stacia clicked off the light and walked slowly to her suitcase. She picked up the car keys that she'd dropped beside the suitcase and touched the house key. She had her own house key, but it was home on her dresser. She'd always carried it to school with her because she had to let herself in after school each day. Now she wouldn't have to. She'd come home to Grandma's house. Grandma was always home! And if she wasn't, Grandpa was. Stacia bit back a loud cry of anger.

Just then Dad walked in. He stopped in the middle of the room and pushed his hands into the pockets of his dress pants. He rattled his change and forced a smile. "You'll like having a room and bathroom of your own, Sta."

She wanted to say, "No, I won't." Instead she shrugged.

"I came to say good night and get my keys." He held out his hand.

She gripped the keys so tightly they pressed painfully into her palm. Finally she gave them to Dad. "I don't want to stay here, Daddy," she whispered.

He pulled her close and held her for a long time. He kissed her cheeks and the top of her head. "This was the only thing we could do. We'll be here Saturday morning."

Stacia pulled away and wiped her eyes. Saturday seemed a million years away.

Dad cleared his throat. "Good night, Sta. Remember to read your Bible and pray before you go to bed."

Stacia pressed her lips tightly together. The family always read the Bible and prayed together! How could she do it alone?

Dad kissed Stacia again, said good night awkwardly, then walked out.

Stacia stood in the middle of the room without moving. She smelled his aftershave long after he left.

A few minutes later Mom stopped outside the door, then walked in. "Want me to help you unpack?"

Stacia shook her head. "I want to go home with you."

"I'm sorry, but you can't."

"Please?"

Mom blinked away tears and shook her head. "Please! Please! I'll be good!"

Mom pulled Stacia close. "It's all decided. You're staying here so you can go to school here. We'll be back Saturday."

Stacia clung to Mom, who smelled like mint and felt soft and warm. "I don't want to stay, Mom."

"You must." Mom suddenly looked very businesslike. She held Stacia away from her. "I want you to obey your grandparents, do your homework, and read your Bible and pray every day. We'll pray for you every single day."

Stacia doubled her fists. Why should she read her Bible and pray or obey or do her homework? If Mom and Dad didn't want her any longer, then she didn't have to do what they said.

"Good night, Stacia. I love you." Mom kissed Stacia, then hurried away.

Stacia stood in the middle of the big bedroom for a long, long time.

4

Stacia's First Day

Roxie glanced in the mirror one last time, brushed her hair again, then frowned. Her hair was too short! Chelsea and Hannah could braid theirs or wear ponytails or leave it hanging long. "Why'd I decide I wanted short hair?"

She twisted this way and that to see if her red blouse looked as pretty as she wanted it to. She tucked it in better and tightened the belt in her jeans. "I guess I can't turn into a beautiful woman overnight." How she wished she could! After sitting with Roy Marks in the gym last night, she wanted to do anything to make sure he talked to her and sat with her again. Maybe he'd start liking her instead of Kathy. Roxie flushed. How could she do that to Kathy? Roxie sighed, then shrugged. Kathy liked Ty, so she wouldn't care if Roy stopped liking her.

"Hurry up, Roxie," Eli shouted from the kitchen.

"Coming!" Roxie smiled. Her brother Eli was almost sixteen, and they'd become friends during the summer when she'd taken time to get to know him. She was still trying to make friends with Lacy, who would be seventeen in a few days. Sometimes it didn't seem worth the effort. Lacy always talked about boys and her job and what she was going to do after high school and college.

Roxie ran to the kitchen just as Eli and Lacy left by the back door. Roxie hugged Mom and hurried out to see if she could catch Hannah or Chelsea. Kathy lived outside The Ravines, but she rode the same bus. Roxie looked past the trees covered with red and gold leaves to Hannah's house across the street. Most of the time Hannah had to walk to the bus stop with her three little sisters. This morning Hannah wasn't in sight. Roxie ran down the sidewalk and stopped at the end of the walk leading to Chelsea's house. She wasn't in sight either. They'd probably left already so they wouldn't have to run to the bus stop. They didn't like to look windblown or to smell sweaty.

Just then Roxie spotted Stacia walking down the sidewalk on Hannah's side of the street. Roxie pressed her lips tightly together and scowled. Why was *she* here? She didn't live at The Ravines. There weren't any empty houses in the area, so a new family couldn't have moved in. So where had Stacia come from?

Stacia glanced up just then and saw Roxie. Stacia stopped short, then hurried on, her head down. Roxie Shoulders lived near Grandma and Grandpa! How awful!

Roxie stayed on her side of the street and walked faster. The chilly wind blew against her, but she felt hot all over. Was it possible Stacia was actually going to ride the bus and be in the same school?

Stacia walked faster, her eyes straight ahead on the crowd of boys and girls waiting at the end of the street. Their laughter floated to her on the wind. Their bright clothes looked like the color of fall trees. In Braselton the colors were drab and gray and dirty. In Braselton she'd be running down dirty streets trying to avoid the gang of boys that hung out on the corner near the rundown apartment buildings between her house and the school.

Roxie ran the last several yards to the edge of the crowd where the Best Friends stood.

Her cheeks as red as her hair, Chelsea caught Roxie's arm. "Did you hear what happened?"

"Again!" Hannah's black eyes were wide in horror.

"What?" Roxie shivered.

"Somebody broke another garage window," Chelsea said. "The Wirts'!"

Roxie gasped. The Wirts lived right across the street from her and right beside Hannah.

"My dad said it probably happened while we

were at school for Parents' Day." Chelsea shivered. "Nobody better break *our* garage windows!"

"That's the fifth window broken at The Ravines," Hannah said with a thoughtful look. Her pulse leaped at the marvelous opportunity to solve a mystery! "I'm going to investigate and try to solve the case."

Kathy giggled. "You sound just like a detective on TV."

Grinning, Hannah shrugged. "What can I say? I like solving mysteries."

"We know," Chelsea, Roxie, and Kathy said together, then laughed.

Just then Hannah glanced back and spotted Stacia. "Look who's here!" Hannah whispered excitedly to the Best Friends.

Roxie didn't look. She knew Hannah was talking about Stacia.

Hannah smiled and walked right up to Stacia. "Hi. We saw you last night at the middle school, but we didn't know you lived around here. My name's Hannah Shigwam. That's Chelsea McCrea, Kathy Aber, and Roxie Shoulders."

"Hi," Stacia said in a low voice. She wanted to walk away from the girls, but her legs suddenly felt too weak.

"Do you live around here?" Chelsea asked.

Anger rushed through Stacia, and she lifted her

chin. Wind tugged at her long frizzy hair. "I live in Braselton! I would never live in Middle Lake!"

"Then why are you going to school here?" Hannah asked softly.

Stacia hated the answer, but she said it anyway. "I'm staying with my grandparents, but I'll only be here for a while." She would not think about being there until the end of the school year. It was too awful to consider.

"Who are your grandparents?" Chelsea asked.

"Parleen and Arnold Smith."

"I've met them," Hannah said. "Your grandma grows some really pretty flowers."

Stacia only shrugged. She didn't want to talk about Grandma or her flowers.

Smiling, Hannah stepped closer to Stacia. "Would you like to sit with us on the bus?"

Stacia started to nod, then shook her head. "I'd rather sit by myself."

"Naturally," Roxie muttered under her breath.

Stacia walked away, her head high and her shoulders square.

"She's stuck up," Roxie hissed. "I say, let's ignore her."

"She's frightened and lonely," Hannah said softly. "And I'm going to make friends with her." Looking very determined, Hannah hurried after Stacia.

Roxie made a face, then turned to Chelsea.

"Did the Wirts call the police about the broken window?"

"Yes. But the police said they probably wouldn't be able to discover who broke them. They said it's probably kids, and they don't think they'll be able to find out who unless they catch them in the act."

Smiling dreamily, Kathy hugged her school books to her. The broken windows didn't affect her since she lived outside The Ravines, and she was getting bored hearing about them. "Can we talk about something interesting? Like Ty Wilton."

Chelsea shook her head. "You said you'd forget about him."

"No, I didn't."

Roxie took a deep breath. "What about Roy Marks? I thought you liked him."

Kathy shook her head. "He's too young!"

"He's in sixth grade with us!"

"I know." Kathy tossed her head. "Way too young!"

"I think he's nice," Chelsea said.

"Me too." Roxie's heart raced. "And he's really smart."

Just then the bus screeched to a stop, and the mass of students piled on. Roxie sat with Chelsea and Kathy. Hannah sat with Stacia.

On the way to school Hannah told Stacia about the broken garage windows and other things that had happened in the neighborhood—tipped-over garbage cans and dented aluminum siding on homes and other terrible acts of vandalism.

Stacia sat back and let Hannah talk. It wouldn't do any good to tell her to be quiet. Stacia didn't care about the broken windows or anything else about The Ravines. She wanted to go home where she belonged, even if it meant going to Braselton Middle School.

Hannah knew Stacia wasn't really listening, but she talked anyway. Silently she prayed Stacia would have a good day and not feel lonely or sad.

■

At school Roxie watched Hannah walk Stacia to the office to get her list of classes, then turned to say something to Kathy. But she was already across the hall talking to Ty. Chelsea had hurried to her locker to get her homework.

Roy Marks walked past just then. He wore a blue shirt and jeans. He stopped short when he saw Kathy with Ty.

"Hi, Roy," Roxie said softly.

Roy managed a smile as he walked to her side. "Hi, Roxie. You going to reading?"

"Uh huh." Roxie wanted to say a whole lot more, but she couldn't think of a thing. Her face suddenly felt hot.

"I'll walk with you." Roy fell into step beside her, and they walked to reading without speaking.

Stacia left the office with Hannah. The noise in the hall was different than at Braselton. Here the noise was only lockers banging and students laughing and talking. There weren't guards yelling and searching lockers for weapons or students swearing and fighting.

"There are only ten blacks in sixth grade," Hannah said.

Stacia acted as if she hadn't heard. Braselton Middle School had mostly African Americans, a few Hispanics, and a few whites.

A black girl smiled at Stacia and said hi. Stacia lifted her chin and wouldn't smile or say hello. She pressed her lips tightly together. No way would she make friends in this new school! If she made friends, Mom and Dad might think she wanted to stay forever.

Hannah led the way to the homeroom.

Stacia bit back a moan as she found an empty seat. Would Mom and Dad make her stay forever?

Mr. Borgman looked around the room until finally everyone grew quiet. He smiled at Stacia, then said in his deep gravel-like voice, "Class, please welcome our new student, Stacia King."

Roxie rolled her eyes. King! That figured. She acted like she was royalty!

"I'm Mr. Borgman, your homeroom teacher as well as reading, English, and social studies teacher.

Right now we're reading Chapter 8 in our readers. Roy, please give Stacia a brief account of the story."

With chills of delight running up and down her back, Roxie sat up straight and watched the back of Roy's head as he talked. He was sooo cute! Last night she'd made sure she brushed her hand against his three times while they sat together in the gym. Several girls in her class asked boys to go with them, but she didn't have the courage. Roy might say no.

Stacia listened to Roy for a minute, then let her mind drift. She'd already read the story and taken a test on it in her school. English was the first hour at Braselton. Miss Lemon was the teacher. Most of the kids called her Miss Sour, but Stacia never had because she liked Miss Lemon. Stacia laced her pencil through her fingers. She'd even thought about becoming a teacher. But mostly she wanted to be a famous gospel singer like Stacia Robedioux, the woman she'd been named after. Stacia rested her chin in her hands and stared at the back of Roy's head without seeing it. In April the whole family had gone to hear Stacia Robedioux in Lansing. It had been sooo incredible! She'd felt the music to the bottoms of her feet and had almost danced when Stacia Robedioux had.

Suddenly Stacia realized that now she wouldn't be able to spend Friday nights singing with Lorraine Browne. They'd been practicing one of Stacia Robedioux's songs to sing in church in November.

Tears burned Stacia's eyes, and she blinked fast to keep from crying. Lorraine would probably get Rana Ayers to sing instead. Stacia leaned back in her seat and closed her eyes tight. Rana sang flat on all the high notes—she always had and she probably always would!

After reading class Stacia looked at her class assignments, then headed for math class.

"Stacia, wait for me." Smiling, Hannah hurried over to her new friend. "We don't have assigned seats in math, so we can sit together."

Stacia shrugged. She wanted to tell Hannah to leave her alone, but she didn't bother. Hannah would soon get tired of the Good Samaritan act.

The day dragged for Stacia. In social studies she heard only a little of what Mr. Borgman said. She did hear him say something about a special assignment though.

"The assignment is due in two weeks."

Hannah raised her hand. "I'd like to be partners with Stacia King for the assignment."

Stacia sat up straight. Just what was the assignment, and why did they need partners?

Mr. Borgman looked at Stacia. "Is that all right with you?"

She shrugged. "Sure. Why not?"

Hannah smiled. It would be fun to work with Stacia and get to know her. It would be easy to work together too since they lived so close to each other. Maybe they could even have sleepovers.

Stacia stared down at her book. Whatever the special assignment was, she wasn't going to do it. So what if she failed the class? Who'd care anyway? She glanced at Hannah, then quickly looked away. This wasn't the time to think about how Hannah would feel.

Later, on the bus Stacia sat beside two little girls at the front just so she wouldn't have to sit with Hannah.

Roxie watched Stacia, then turned to Hannah. "Don't bother with her, Hannah. She doesn't want to be friends."

Hannah smiled and shrugged. "She's sad and lonely and scared. I intend to be her friend."

Roxie rolled her eyes and shook her head.

"One of the Best Friends' rules is to be a friend to others. That's even in the Bible." Hannah hooked her long hair behind her ears. "I intend to do that, no matter what."

At the front of the bus Stacia stared out the window at the line of trees covered with bright red and gold and orange leaves. In Braselton there weren't any trees! "I don't care! I still want to go home," she said under her breath. Somehow she'd find a way to make Mom and Dad take her back.

5

King's Kids

Chelsea sat in the middle of the rec room on the floor in her basement and looked at the Best Friends. She'd called a *King's Kids* meeting to discuss new business—namely, should Stacia King be invited to join? During the summer they'd met outdoors, but it was too chilly now. The rec room was a perfect place to meet, especially if they wanted to play games, watch the big-screen TV, or have a snack afterwards.

She'd started the *King's Kids* to make money to pay for the outrageous phone bill she'd built up when she first moved from Oklahoma to Michigan. Other kids wanted to work odd jobs too, so she'd formed the business and named it *King's Kids*. Jesus was their King, and they all loved Him. Chelsea pushed back her long red hair. She was the president since she'd started the business, Hannah the treasurer because she was good with money, Roxie the secretary since she had the best handwriting, and Kathy the vice president because it was the only office left.

Suddenly Chelsea laughed. "Stacia *King—King's Kids*. Isn't that funny? I say she fits right in."

Hannah lifted her hand and nodded in agreement. "So do I."

Chelsea turned to Roxie and Kathy. "How do you two vote?"

Kathy had been daydreaming about Ty, so she hadn't heard a word. "Vote for what?"

"I say no," Roxie snapped. "I don't like Stacia at all. She doesn't like anybody but herself. She wouldn't be a good *King's Kid*."

Kathy frowned. "What are you talking about?"

Chelsea jabbed Kathy's leg. "Listen, will you? We're voting to see if we should invite Stacia King to be a *King's Kid*."

Kathy laughed. "Stacia King—*King's Kids*. Funny, eh?"

The others groaned. Chelsea jumped up. "I say let's ask Stacia if she wants to join. If you agree, raise your hand."

Chelsea, Hannah, and Kathy lifted their hands. Roxie sat on hers.

"The majority rules." Chelsea dropped back down. "We'll ask Stacia to join."

"I'll ask her," Hannah said eagerly. "She'll

want to join after I tell her how great it is. And she might be glad to earn some extra money."

"I wonder why she lives with her grandparents." Chelsea flopped on her stomach and rested her arms on a fat white pillow. Her red hair hung down on the pillow—flame red against bright white. "I love my grandparents, but I wouldn't want to live with them or go to school near them."

Roxie hugged her legs to her chest. "I'd hate to go to a different school. I wouldn't get to see . . . all my friends." She'd almost said, "Roy Marks."

Kathy sighed and smiled dreamily. "I wouldn't get to see Ty or talk to him or pass notes in the hall."

Hannah frowned at Kathy. "What about cheerleading? You said that was the most important thing in your life."

"That was before Ty."

"You'd better stop thinking about him so much," Chelsea warned. "Remember the Scripture that says to shun the very appearance of evil."

"You don't have to keep talking about that, do you?" Kathy twisted a blonde curl around her finger. "You girls are making me mad! Ty is not evil!"

"No, but he's not a Christian," Hannah said sternly.

"Just drop it," Kathy snapped. She hated to have the girls disagree with her.

Roxie popped open a bag of tortilla chips and passed the bag around. The noise of the plastic bag and crunching chips was loud for a while. She swallowed a big bite and looked at the Best Friends. "If you could go with any boy you wanted, who would you go with?"

"Ty Wilton," Kathy said before anyone else had a chance to speak.

"But you can't go with him, and you know it." Hannah shook her head. "He's not a Christian."

Kathy lifted her chin. "Roxie said if we could go with anyone. *If!* So I said Ty."

"That's right. She did say *if*." Chelsea sat up and pulled the pillow onto her lap. "I'd go with . . . Brody Vangaar."

Kathy gasped in shock. "My foster brother? You'd go with him?"

Chelsea grinned and nodded. "I love to hear him play guitar and sing. And he's sooo cute!"

"I can't believe you'd go with him!" Kathy shook her head and looked at Chelsea as if she were from another planet.

Roxie nudged Hannah. "What about you?"

Hannah flushed. Boys usually stayed away from her because she wasn't white. "I really don't know."

"What?" Chelsea giggled and shook her head. "Come on, Hannah, you must like somebody. Who is he?"

"Tell us. Tell us!" they all chorused.

"Who, Hannah?" Roxie urged.

She took a deep breath. It was very hard for her to share such a personal thing, even with the Best Friends, but since they were her best friends, she would. She trembled. "I'd go with . . . with . . . Eli Shoulders."

Roxie choked on the chip in her mouth. She coughed so hard, Chelsea had to slap her on the back to keep her from choking.

Hannah flushed. "I know you think it's awful for an Ottawa to like your brother, Roxie."

"She doesn't think that at all!" Chelsea shook her head hard. "Do you?"

Roxie hung her head. She'd thought exactly that. "I'm sorry," she said just above a whisper. "I thought I'd gotten over being prejudiced, but I guess I haven't. I'm really really sorry, Hannah."

"That's all right." Hannah blinked back hot tears. Why did others think she was different just because she was Ottawa? Finally she managed to smile. "What about you, Roxie? You didn't tell us who you'd go with."

"Tell us. Tell us," Chelsea and Kathy said together.

A shiver trickled down Roxie's spine. If she told, would Kathy get angry? Would Chelsea and Hannah think she was terrible for liking the boy Kathy had considered hers?

"Come on, Roxie! Tell us!"

Roxie cleared her throat. "Roy," she whispered.

"Roy who?" Kathy asked.

Roxie's neck and face burned. "Roy Marks."

"No!" Kathy jumped up, her fists doubled at her sides. "That's not fair, Roxie Shoulders, and you know it!"

Her eyes flashing, Roxie sprang to her feet. "And why not? You said you like Ty." Roxie turned to Chelsea and Hannah. "Didn't she? How can she like two boys?"

Kathy burst into tears. "I can't believe you're doing this to me, Roxie. I thought we were best friends!"

"We are," Hannah said quickly. "Don't fight over a boy. Let's talk about something else. Like how to help Stacia King."

Roxie ran to the stairs, then turned and glared at everyone. "I won't help Her Majesty! I mean it!" Roxie spun around and leaped up the steps two at a time. She ran out the back door and across the yard to her house. Then she remembered Chelsea hadn't ended the meeting. Roxie tossed her head and slowed down when she came to the walk that led up to her door. "Too bad!"

■

Down the street Stacia King stood at the kitchen sink and filled several glasses with water.

"Please hurry, Stacia," Grandma said as she put

a bowl of mashed potatoes on the table. "Grandpa wants to eat before the news comes on."

Stacia wanted to snap, "Too bad!" But she quickly filled the glasses and carried them to the table. Smells of roast beef, mashed potatoes, buttered corn, and fresh yeast rolls made her stomach growl. She frowned impatiently. She couldn't understand how she could be so hungry when she was so unhappy.

Grandma set the butter dish near Grandpa's plate. "Get your grandpa. He's in the basement working on a song."

Stacia reluctantly walked to the basement door, hesitated, then walked down the steps. Grandpa had built a soundproof studio so he could practice piano and trumpet without bothering anyone. Stacia stopped outside the door. Grandpa hated to be interrupted when he was in his studio. She knocked softly, waited, then knocked again.

Grandpa flung the door open. He'd changed from his dirty work clothes to a clean pair of jeans and a blue and red pullover shirt with long sleeves. "What do you want?" He sounded gruff, and he looked angry.

"Supper's on."

"Get on up. I'll be right there." He closed the door with a bang.

Stacia swallowed hard, then ran across the carpeted floor to the stairs. It was hard to imagine

Grandpa loving music. He worked in a factory all day long and had for years. Mom had said Grandpa never told anyone at work or at church about his love for music or that he'd once had his own band and been on the road with it almost five years. He'd had to stop when he and Grandma had kids. Maybe that was why Grandpa was such a grouch.

Impatiently Stacia pushed aside thoughts of Grandpa. She didn't care if he was a grouch or not. She'd stay as far away from him as she always had.

A few minutes later Stacia finished the meal that was so different from the noisy ones at home, then helped Grandma clean the kitchen while Grandpa sat in the living room and watched the news. The loud TV and the whirr of the dishwasher were the only sounds. Finally Stacia was able to run upstairs to her room.

She looked out the window at other homes. Some of them already had their lights on. She thought about Lorraine Browne and the practices they'd miss. Maybe they could practice Saturday or Sunday afternoon. She thought about it a long time, then nodded. "I'll call her," Stacia whispered.

Afraid she'd lose her nerve, she hurried to Grandpa and Grandma's bedroom to use the phone there. The bedspread was a cream-colored crocheted one that hung unevenly over the bed. The room smelled like medicine. Stacia picked up the phone, her heart thundering. It was long-distance, and she knew it cost extra to call, but she just had to talk to Lorraine.

Lorraine answered on the third ring. Stacia's heart hammered, and her hand felt sweaty.

"Hi. It's me."

"Stacia! Your mom told me about you staying with your grandparents. Are you there now?"

"Yes."

"Hey, I'm sorry we can't practice together any longer. Your mom told me."

Stacia's heart sank. "What about Saturdays or Sundays?"

"Sorry, but I can't."

"What'll we do then?"

"I got Rana."

Stacia gripped the receiver so hard, her knuckles hurt. "But she sings off-key!"

Lorraine sighed heavily. "I know. We'll have to work on it."

Tears filled Stacia's eyes and ran down her cheeks. "If I get to come home to live, can we sing together again?"

"Sure . . . Well, I don't know. It really wouldn't be fair to Rana, you know?"

"What about me, Lorraine? Is it fair to me?"

"I'm real sorry," Lorraine said in a small voice. "Really. Your mom said you'd be gone until June when school's out."

Stacia bit her lip. "I gotta go. Bye." She hung

up and ran to her room. Until June! No way! She paced the bedroom, her hands locked at her racing heart.

"Stacia!" Grandma called up the stairs. "Phone for you. You can take it in my bedroom."

Stacia tried to rub away her tears as she ran to her grandparents' bedroom. Maybe it was Mom saying she could come home after all. She scooped up the phone and answered breathlessly.

"Hi, Stacia. This is Hannah Shigwam."

Anger rushed through Stacia. "What do you want?"

Hannah froze, then said softly, "Is something wrong?"

"Should there be?"

"I know you're lonely and sad. I'm praying for you."

Stacia's heart jerked, and then she frowned. "Don't bother!"

"It's no bother. I called to tell you about *King's Kids* and to talk about our school project, but I can tell you're not in the mood, so I'll talk to you tomorrow."

"Just leave me alone, will you?"

Hannah twisted the phone cord and almost hung up, then remembered the real reason Stacia was upset. "See ya tomorrow, Stacia. Good night. Remember, Jesus is always with you."

Stacia dropped the receiver in place, then covered her face with her hands. Jesus had always taken care of her, but this time He had forgotten her, just like Mom and Dad had.

Slowly Stacia walked to her room, closed the door, and leaned against it.

6

Friend or Foe

Her pulse leaping, Roxie waited near Roy's locker. She tried to act as if she weren't waiting for him. Her cheeks felt on fire. Smells of coffee and perfume wove in and out among the laughing, shouting, and talking students rushing up and down the hall. Thankfully no one noticed her or asked her what she was doing. Since she'd put her carvings on display, students spoke to her who never had before. Having so many people take notice of her was very embarrassing. She'd be glad when she could take her work home and set it on the shelf in her room. She patted her flushed cheeks and tried to act as if she were going somewhere, not just waiting for Roy.

Finally she spotted Roy, and her heart almost jumped out of her chest. He wore a school jacket, gray shirt, loose-fitting jeans, and white sneakers. His hair looked as if he'd just combed it. Was he trying to look extra-nice for her?

Trying to act nonchalant, Roxie shifted her books in her arms and walked toward Roy. When she was almost next to him she said brightly, "Hi, Roy! How are you this morning?"

"Hi, Roxie." He stopped beside her and looked around until he spotted Kathy with Ty. He frowned. "I could be better."

Roxie's smile froze. She touched his arm, sending a thrill over her. It didn't seem to do much at all for him though. He probably hadn't even noticed her touch. "Forget Kathy, Roy."

"I can't," he whispered.

"But she likes Ty." Roxie's stomach knotted, and she felt bad for what she was doing, but she pushed away the guilty thoughts and continued, "She liked you for a while, but now she likes you only as a friend."

Roy's face fell.

"I'm sorry." But she wasn't sorry at all, and she wished she hadn't said that.

Roy pushed his hands deep into the pockets of his jeans. "Why does she like him instead of me? He's a real jerk!"

"I know. But Kathy doesn't think he is."

"Maybe she'll realize it and like me again."

Roxie's heart dropped. This was not going like she'd planned! "I don't think she will. Really. She likes Ty a lot, even if he is a jerk." Roxie turned so she couldn't see Kathy. "She'll like Ty for a long time. I know Kathy. She makes up her mind, and she doesn't change it."

Roy hung his head. "What'll I do?"

Roxie shrugged. "Forget her. There are other girls, you know." Like me, she wanted to say.

Roy tugged at his jacket. "Did you know I used to take toys from Kathy in kindergarten just to tease her?"

Roxie nodded as she shifted from one foot to the other. She'd hoped Roy would be glad to talk to her and even walk to class with her. But she couldn't handle having him talk about Kathy!

Roy sighed as he walked to his locker. "I liked her even then, but I didn't know how to tell her."

Roxie wanted to slap his arm and tell him to quit wasting his time on Kathy. "That's all past now."

"I know." Roy opened his locker and hung up his jacket. "I guess I should've been nicer to her. I shouldn't have teased her so much last month. But it scared me to talk to her."

"Don't think about it, Roy. It's too late." Roxie stepped closer to Roy. "Let's walk to class."

"Sure. Okay. I guess we should." Roy smiled weakly. "You're a good friend, Rox."

Roxie gripped her books. How she hated to be called Rox! Next he'd call her Stone the way he had all last year.

She glanced over her shoulder. Kathy was

frowning at her. Flushing, she turned back. She hesitated, then fell into step with Roy. Kathy had no business frowning just because she was with Roy. "Maybe we could sit together at lunch?"

"Sure. Okay."

Roxie's heart leaped. She walked into class, then glanced back. Kathy looked ready to cry. Roxie turned quickly around and pushed all thoughts of Kathy away.

■

Stacia sank to her seat and hunched her shoulders. Her hair fell forward, hiding her face. She hadn't slept much last night. Her grandparents' house had felt different than hers. Her sisters weren't beside her snoring or mumbling in their sleep. And the street sounds were quieter here. At times she'd even heard a dog bark.

Hannah stopped at Stacia's desk. "Morning!"

Stacia glanced up, then quickly down at her desktop.

"How are you today?"

Stacia's eyes pricked with tears at the kindness she heard in Hannah's voice. Stacia forced back the tears and lifted her chin haughtily. "I'm perfectly fine. Shouldn't I be?"

Hannah took a step back, then managed a smile. She knew how Stacia felt inside no matter how ugly she acted. "Let's have lunch together, okay?"

Stacia frowned. "I might not eat."

"I'll meet you right outside the science room, and we'll walk together." Hannah smiled, then rushed to her seat before Stacia could say no.

Stacia locked her hands in her lap and stared straight ahead. Why was Hannah so persistent?

At lunchtime Stacia tried to sneak past Hannah, but she didn't make it.

"I'm really hungry," Hannah said with a cheery smile. "I got up kind of late this morning and only had time for a piece of toast. Do you like a big or small breakfast?"

Stacia's throat closed over. Why wouldn't Hannah leave her alone? She walked around three sixth-grade boys who were arguing about a soccer score. The smell of pizza drifted out of the cafeteria.

Hannah hurried after Stacia. Hannah didn't speak again until she sat at the end of a table with Stacia. Two boys sat at the other end, acting as if they were alone.

"I'm working on a mystery," Hannah said in a low voice so the boys couldn't hear.

Stacia's pulse leaped, but she didn't let Hannah know she was interested.

Hannah told Stacia about the vandalizing at The Ravines. "I asked the families a few questions, but I'm going to see if I can find clues. I might even stake a garage out to see if I can catch the culprit in the act."

Stacia giggled, then frowned because she'd dared to let her feelings show. She bit off a huge bite of pizza and chewed it so she wouldn't be able to speak.

Hannah ate her pizza and drank the strawberry shake. She knew she'd finally caught Stacia's interest. "I'll come see you after school, and we can investigate together."

Stacia nodded before she could stop herself. She scowled and jumped up. "I might not be home." Maybe Mom and Dad would miss her so much they'd take her home yet tonight.

"I'll stop by just in case."

Her ears burning, Stacia hurried out of the cafeteria.

■

Across the cafeteria Roxie moved a little closer to Roy without seeming to. She'd eaten the pizza without tasting it while Roy talked on and on about Kathy. Twice Roxie had almost blurted out for him to quit talking about Kathy, but she'd lost her nerve. If she wouldn't let him talk about Kathy, he might not want to sit with her again.

Finally she blurted out the first thing that popped into her head. "Have you met Stacia King, the new girl?"

"No. Have you?"

"Sure. She lives at The Ravines. Did you hear about the vandalism there?"

Roy shook his head but didn't seem interested at all.

Roxie finally excused herself and rushed to the restroom before class started. Tears blurred her vision, and she wanted to burst into tears. Why couldn't Roy forget about Kathy? It wasn't fair!

After school Roxie clicked the lock on her locker, but it wouldn't open. She shouldn't have waited for Roy. When she'd finally seen him, he'd been with George Bender. They'd walked past her as if she were invisible. She'd wanted to call to Roy, but the words stuck in her throat.

She scowled. Why couldn't she ever get her locker open when she was late? It would be terrible if she missed the bus and had to call her mom to pick her up. She carefully tried the lock again, being careful to hit each number of the combination. This time it opened. Breathing a sigh of relief, she shoved the books she didn't need inside and ran down the empty hall and out into the sunshine. She raced for the bus and reached it just as the driver started to close the door. Breathlessly she hurried down the aisle. Boys and girls talked and laughed. The only empty seat was beside Kathy. Roxie's heart sank. She hesitated, then dropped down beside her just as the bus jerked forward.

Kathy crossed her arms and stared out the window. She should've let Marla Perkins sit there when she'd tried. Roxie might even think she'd saved the seat for her. Kathy glanced at Roxie, then quickly away.

Roxie jabbed Kathy's arm. "What's wrong with you?" she asked innocently.

"Nothing. Should there be?"

Roxie thought about the look Kathy had given her when she and Roy were together. "Of course not."

"Then why'd you ask?" The bus turned a corner, and Kathy fell against Roxie. Kathy pulled quickly away. "Are you feeling guilty for flirting with Roy?"

Roxie frowned. "Guilty? Me? Why should I?" But she did.

"Because Roy likes me, not you!"

"But you don't like him, and it's not fair to keep him thinking you do."

Kathy twisted a blonde curl around her finger. "I didn't say I don't like him. It's just that Ty is really really great."

"He is not! Roy is!"

Kathy leaned against the seat and closed her eyes. "I don't want to fight, Roxie. Do you?"

Roxie shook her head. "I hate fighting. Especially with a best friend." She was silent until a group of kids got off the bus, and it pulled away from the curb. "We are still best friends, aren't we?"

"Sure . . . I guess so." Kathy bit her lip. She didn't feel like a friend at all.

"I guess you want me to stay away from Roy."

"Of course!"

Roxie shook her head. "I can't," she whispered.

Kathy's temper flared, and she snapped her mouth closed before she said the hateful words rising inside her.

Roxie locked her hands in her lap and pressed her lips together. She didn't dare speak or she knew she'd say something she'd be sorry for later.

The bus stopped near Kathy's home. Without a good-bye she slipped past Roxie and hurried down the aisle. She ran down the sidewalk to her house and slipped inside. Suddenly she remembered she had a *King's Kids* job to do—planting tulip bulbs with Roxie at Ezra Menski's. "I won't go! Roxie can do it alone." Kathy sighed heavily. She knew she couldn't stay home. One of the rules as a *King's Kid* was to always do the job you'd agreed to do unless something major came up. Being mad at Roxie wasn't major.

Kathy ran to her room to change into old jeans and a sweatshirt.

At her house Roxie slammed her bedroom door. She felt like crawling into bed and pulling the cover over her head. She jerked off her school clothes. Suddenly she remembered she had to plant bulbs for Ezra Menski, the man her grandma had married last month. But worse yet, Kathy was going to work with her.

Roxie yanked on her old jeans and pulled on a faded blue T-shirt. She saw her *I'm A Best Friend* button on her desk. She picked it up and shoved it to the back of her desk drawer. She might have to work with Kathy, but she sure wasn't going to wear that button!

Maybe she could call Chelsea and ask to have someone else take the job. "She'll never agree," Roxie muttered as she rushed out the bedroom door. Chelsea believed in following the *King's Kids* rules, especially since she'd made them up.

Roxie ran to the kitchen and pulled out the peanut butter to make a sandwich. Maybe she could be late for the job. She wrinkled her nose and shook her head. Being on time was another rule. She wolfed down her sandwich, drank a glass of milk, then hurried outside. How could she work with Kathy without yelling at her? Well, working with Kathy was a lot better than working with Stacia King. "I'll make sure I never have to do that!" she vowed.

7

The Investigation

Roxie stopped outside Ezra Menski's door. He was her grandpa now, but she usually couldn't bring herself to call him that. Her grandpa was in Heaven with Jesus.

"Aren't they home?" Kathy asked as she leaned her bike against the side of the porch.

"I didn't knock yet."

Kathy frowned. "Well, knock! We don't want to take all evening, you know."

With her lips pressed together to keep back angry words, Roxie knocked on the door. It opened immediately, and she jumped back.

"Roxann!" Grandma hugged Roxie tight. Grandma wore black pants, a white blouse, and a black and white bulky sweater. "Hello, Kathy. Ezra had to go downtown, but he told me where he wants the bulbs planted."

Roxie smelled Grandma's rose perfume. Today

68

it didn't bother her that Grandma called her Roxann. Grandma and Ezra were the only ones who ever did.

"We're ready to work," Kathy said, smiling. It was hard to get used to calling Roxie's grandma Mrs. Menski instead of Mrs. Potter. Maybe she'd stay to watch them. Kathy peeked at Roxie. She didn't want to be alone with Roxie and start fighting again.

Emma Menski led the girls to the front walk and pointed to the flower bed between the sidewalk and the curb. "Ezra had tulips in here before and wants you to plant more bulbs there." She told them how deep to plant them and which end to put up. "We don't want them to grow upside-down." She chuckled and patted the girls on their arms. "You'll find the bulbs and the tools in the garage."

"Are you going to stay with us to make sure we do it right?" Roxie asked.

Emma shook her head. "I have a cake in the oven. But I'll be out later to see how you're doing."

Roxie's heart sank. She'd wanted Grandma to stay. It would be hard to be alone with Kathy. She probably felt the same way.

Emma hurried back inside while Roxie and Kathy walked into the garage. It smelled like gasoline. Roxie found the red plastic bucket full of tulip bulbs, and Kathy picked up the bulb planters and the rake. As they stepped back out into the sunshine, Hannah and Stacia walked up to the garage.

Roxie greeted Hannah but ignored Stacia.

"Did you come to help?" Kathy asked, hoping they had.

Hannah shook her head. "We're investigating the vandalism. Has Ezra had any trouble?"

Roxie shook her head. "Not that I know of."

Stacia moved restlessly. She hated being around Roxie. Stacia looked at the bucket of bulbs, at the trees lining the street, then down at the ground. She should've refused to come with Hannah. Maybe Mom planned to call and now she'd miss talking to her.

"We have to hurry. Let's talk while we work." Roxie hurried to the spot and knelt down. The sooner she finished, the sooner she could leave.

Kathy hurried after Roxie and laid the bulbs out in the places where they would plant them.

Hannah stood on the sidewalk with Stacia beside her. A cat rubbed against her ankles, then ambled off across the street. "I forgot to tell you about *King's Kids*, Stacia."

Stacia shrugged. She didn't care if she learned anything more about the girls. She watched a boy ride past on his bike as a dog barked furiously at him and chased the rear tire. Why couldn't she just walk away and leave Hannah to do what she wanted?

Hannah hesitated, knowing Stacia really wasn't interested in *King's Kids*, but she told her how they'd started anyway. "So we thought you might like to sign up to work too."

Stacia's head spun with a whole new idea. Maybe she could work hard and make enough money for the family to move so she could go home again. "Sure, I'll sign up to work. When can I start? Today?"

Hannah chuckled. She'd expected Stacia to refuse. "We'll talk to Chelsea. She assigns the jobs."

Kathy jumped up. "You could take over for me if you want."

"Sure. Okay."

Roxie glared at Kathy. "You know she can't. Did you forget the rules?"

Hannah quickly explained the rules to Stacia. "So you really can't take over for Kathy even if you want to. Sorry."

Stacia peeked at Roxie through her lashes. Had Roxie refused her offer because she was African American?

With Stacia beside her, Hannah started to walk away, then stopped. "Are you sure no one has tried to break Ezra's garage windows?"

"We don't know," Roxie and Kathy said at the same time.

Roxie pushed the bulb planter deep into the soft soil. "Ask my grandma."

"I will." Hannah ran lightly up the steps to the front door and knocked.

Stacia looked longingly down the street. She wanted to see Chelsea right now and get a job assigned to her. Reluctantly she joined Hannah and waited beside her.

Emma Menski opened the door and smiled. The smell of chocolate cake drifted out along with the sound of taped piano music. "Hello, Hannah. And you must be Stacia King. Welcome to our neighborhood."

Stacia stared at Mrs. Menski in surprise.

"Your grandmother told me today you were staying with them."

They talked a while longer, and then Hannah said, "Has anyone tried to vandalize your garage or the ones on either side of you?"

Emma shook her head. "Ezra thought he heard someone out there a couple of nights ago, but when he looked he couldn't see anyone. Why do you ask?"

Hannah lifted her chin a little. Some people thought she was too young to help solve mysteries, but she knew better. "I'm trying to learn who's been vandalizing The Ravines."

"That could be dangerous, Hannah." Emma patted Hannah's arm. "Be very careful. We don't want anything to happen to you."

"I'll be careful." Hannah said a quick good-bye and hurried away with Stacia close beside her.

"Are we going to see Chelsea now?"

"As soon as we check one more garage for clues. I want to see if there's a pattern or if it's being done at random."

"Are you going to be a detective when you grow up?"

Hannah grinned. "I don't think so. But I might. I like to paint and play the piano too. And I'm good in science. How about you? What do you want to be?"

"A singer." Stacia gasped. Why had she told Hannah? "What does it matter what I want to be? It takes a long time to grow up."

"We can begin to prepare ourselves now, and we can learn all we can too. God has a purpose for each of us. We need to learn what it is, then do it."

Stacia didn't want to listen to that. She wanted to find a way to get home where she belonged.

Hannah stopped at a garage that had had the windows broken out. New windows had already been installed. It was probably too late to find clues. "I guess the trail is dead." She pulled a paper out of the back pocket of her jeans. "I marked where each garage was hit and when. Take a look."

Stacia was interested even though she didn't want to be. "Is there a pattern?"

"I don't think so. Maybe he doesn't decide

where he'll strike until he's there and finds the opportunity."

"He? Or it could be a she, right?"

Hannah's eyes widened. "You're right! I never thought about it being a girl or woman, but it could be. It doesn't take extra strength to break a window or tip over a garbage can."

"Maybe it was Roxie. She doesn't seem very nice."

Hannah shook her head. "It can't be Roxie. She sometimes gets angry, but she'd never do anything like that. She is one of my best friends, you know."

"Oh . . . I didn't know." Stacia ducked her head. "I guess I shouldn't have said anything."

"It's okay. Let's go see Chelsea now." Hannah walked down the sidewalk with Stacia beside her. She told Stacia about the four of them being best friends and about the Best Friends Club they'd formed. "I never had a real friend before Chelsea moved here from Oklahoma. I prayed for a friend, and God gave me three best friends." Hannah brushed tears from her eyes. "I cry every time I think about it."

Tears stung Stacia's eyes, but she wouldn't let Hannah see. Lorraine was her friend—or at least had been before Stacia had been forced to stay with Grandma and Grandpa. When she went back home maybe nobody would even remember her.

A few minutes later Hannah and Stacia sat in

Chelsea's bedroom while Chelsea looked over the available jobs.

"Here's one, Stacia." Chelsea flipped back her long red hair and smiled. "It's baby-sitting for two little girls tomorrow right after school. It's across the street from your grandparents. Can you do it?"

"Maybe they won't want me . . . because I'm black."

"They won't care." Chelsea wrote the information on a card and gave it to Stacia. "We always check out the people who hire us to make sure they're okay. The Grahams are nice, and so are their daughters Kendall and Rochelle. If you have any problems while you're there, call me or Hannah or Roxie. Kathy lives too far away to get to you fast. If none of us are available, call your grandparents for help."

Stacia nodded. No way would she call Roxie, but she might one of the others. Besides, she wouldn't have any problems. She was used to baby-sitting.

A few minutes later Hannah and Stacia told Chelsea good-bye and walked back outdoors.

"Have you thought about our special assignment?" Hannah asked as they waited for a green pickup to pass before they crossed the street.

Stacia shrugged. "There's still time." She wouldn't tell Hannah she didn't even know what the assignment was.

"I guess so. We'll talk about it tomorrow. I have to help fix dinner and maybe watch baby Burke for a while."

Stacia's stomach knotted. How she missed her three little sisters! They were a big pain sometimes, but she loved them.

Several minutes later Stacia walked up the sidewalk to her grandparents' house. Grandma was sitting on the porch.

"Hi, Stacia. I'm resting a bit before I start supper. Grandpa's at the music store buying a new mouthpiece for his trumpet." Grandma patted the spot beside her on the white porch swing. "Come join me."

"I need a drink of water first."

"Would you take a folder of music down to Grandpa's studio? He left it on the kitchen table."

Stacia nodded, then walked inside. She drank a glass of cold water, sighed heavily, and picked up the folder of music. She walked downstairs. It was always cooler in the basement. She laid the folder on Grandpa's desk, then looked around at the mike, the cassette player, and Grandpa's piano. Suddenly she wanted to sing again. There'd been too little music in her life the last few days. She looked over Grandpa's cassette tapes and found one she and Lorraine had practiced many times.

Stacia popped in the cassette and pushed the Play button. She turned on the mike, closed the soundproof door, and waited for her cue. She lifted the mike to her mouth and started to sing. The sound filled the room and seemed to fill her too—with joy! She sang like she'd never sung before. Her nerves tingled, and her soul rejoiced. How she wished Lorraine was singing with her! If they'd been able to practice here in the studio where the acoustics were perfect, they would have been ready to perform in front of the church by now. She could hear each note and know whether she'd hit it or not. For the first time in two days she felt free and happy. Maybe she could tolerate staying here after all if she could practice regularly.

Suddenly the door burst open, and Grandpa stormed in. He clicked off the tape and unplugged the mike. His eyebrows lowered, and fire shot from his eyes. "What are you doing in here? You know you're not allowed!"

"I was only . . . I was only singing," Stacia whispered.

"Get out!" Grandpa pointed to the door. "Get out *now*!"

Her blood cold as ice, Stacia ran out the door and up the stairs. She stumbled on the top step and crashed against the partly open basement door. She bumped her head, sending sudden pain through her entire body. She staggered to her feet and ran out the door. Cold air hit her, and she shivered. She ran down the sidewalk to Hannah's house. Shivering and sobbing, she pressed the doorbell.

Hannah opened the door and gasped. "Stacia! What's wrong? Come in!" Hannah pulled her inside and wrapped her arms around her. Stacia was obviously cold and shaking badly. Silently Hannah prayed for her.

Stacia sobbed against Hannah, then abruptly pulled away. "I don't know why I came."

"Because you know I care." Hannah pushed Stacia's wiry hair away from her damp face. "Please, tell me what's wrong."

Stacia shook her head. "It's not important. Can I use your phone to call my mom? I want to go home."

"Sure. Come in." Hannah locked her arm in Stacia's and walked her to the phone in the hall where she could have privacy. Hannah's little sisters were laughing and talking in the kitchen. Burke cried loudly, then was quiet all at once as if someone had given him something to eat.

Stacia choked back a sob as she dialed the number. "It's long-distance," she said brokenly.

"That's okay. I'll pay for it."

Stacia gripped the receiver and listened while the phone rang and rang. After twelve rings she hung up. "There's no answer." She sobbed, then dabbed at her eyes.

"Maybe they're coming to see you." Hannah handed Stacia a tissue. "They really might."

"Maybe." Stacia blew her nose and crushed the tissue into a paper ball. "I better get back to Grandma's just in case."

"Call me later, okay?" She told Stacia her number.

"I'll try." Stacia started out the door, then turned to Hannah. "Thanks."

Hannah smiled. "Sure. I'll be praying for you."

Stacia hurried away. Lights blazed out of the homes she passed. Streetlights lit the walk. Icy wind blew against her, and she shivered and ran faster.

Three houses away from her grandparents she caught a flash of light near a garage. She stopped short, then ducked behind a tree. Was someone sneaking around a garage and getting ready to break a window? Should she get Hannah?

Stacia shook her head. She had to get home in case Mom and Dad were there. But she didn't move. She watched the light flash again and realized it was someone walking around a garage with a flashlight. She trembled and pressed closer to the rough bark of the tree. A dog barked, and she jumped, scraping her cheek on the bark. She touched her face gingerly. Was the wetness she felt tears or blood?

She peeked around the tree again just as the person with the flashlight disappeared on the far side of the garage. She waited, then hurried down the street.

At the house she looked around for her dad's car. It wasn't there. Her heart sank. Mom and Dad hadn't come! They probably had no intentions of ever getting her!

Just as she turned up the sidewalk she caught sight of a rock decorating the flower garden. She picked it up with both hands. Anger rushed through her, and she threw the rock at the garage. It shattered the window, filling the air with the sound of breaking glass. She gasped and clamped her hand over her mouth. What had she done? Oh, how could she do such a terrible thing?

Her heart hammering, she ran to the back door and slipped inside. She smelled fish and coffee but didn't hear any movement from the kitchen. Cautiously she walked into the empty kitchen, then checked the living room. It was empty too. She saw the basement door open and peeked around it. Grandma and Grandpa were standing at the bottom of the steps with their arms around each other.

Stacia bit her lip. "I'm back," she said.

Grandma looked up with a glad cry.

Grandpa frowned. "It's about time. Supper's ready."

Stacia walked to the kitchen and leaned weakly against the sink.

8

Baby-sitting

Stacia watched at the window until Mrs. Graham drove away, then turned to four-year-old Kendall and three-year-old Rochelle. The two girls were dressed like twins in flowered pants and tops with bright red ribbons in their ponytails. "Want to play in the yard now?"

"Yes!" They jumped up and down and shouted and giggled.

Stacia swallowed the lump in her throat as she helped them on with their small pink jackets. They reminded her of her little sisters when they were younger.

Outdoors in the sunny backyard Kendall ran to the swing set and Rochelle to the canopied sandbox. She brushed the fallen leaves aside and dug in the sand with her little green shovel.

"Push me, Stacia," Kendall called from the swing.

Stacia ran to the swing and pushed Kendall back and forth. Her red ribbons flowed out behind her like tails on a kite.

Rochelle sang a Sunday school song as she filled her pail. She was off-key a little but remembered every word. Stacia smiled. She'd sung the same song many, *many* times.

Just then Stacia heard a noise near the garage. She turned. Her stomach cramped as the picture of her throwing a rock through Grandpa's garage window flashed across her mind. This morning he'd seen it and had called the police. It was on the tip of her tongue to tell him she'd done it, but she feared him so much she just couldn't get it out. Having Grandpa blame the vandals made it easier to keep quiet.

In school today Hannah had already heard about that broken window as well as another not far from there. Stacia gasped. She'd probably seen the vandal last night—the person with the flashlight! She had forgotten about that until just this minute. She'd have to tell Hannah.

Right at that moment Roxie walked out of the Grahams' garage. She stopped short when she saw Stacia. "What are *you* doing here?"

Stacia lifted her chin. "Baby-sitting. Why are you here?"

"Mrs. Graham hired me to work in her garden." Roxie wanted to run home and forget the job, but she knew she couldn't.

Stacia turned away from Roxie and began pushing Kendall again.

"Roxie!" Rochelle dropped her shovel and ran over to Roxie as she walked through the gate and into the backyard.

"Stop me! Stop me!" Kendall cried.

Stacia caught the chains and stopped Kendall. She too raced over to Roxie, joyfully calling her name. Stacia made a face as Roxie hugged the girls and talked to them. She thought about leaving and letting Roxie baby-sit while she worked on the garden. "No way!" Stacia muttered. She needed the money too badly to quit the job.

Roxie finally sent the girls back to play and started cleaning out the flowers the frost had killed. Why hadn't Chelsea told her Stacia was baby-sitting? It was awkward being in the same backyard with her.

Stacia wanted to take the girls inside, but Mrs. Graham had said to let them play outdoors for an hour. "Let's play ring-around-the-rosy, girls." Stacia made her voice sound full of excitement even though she didn't feel like it.

The girls ran to her and caught her hands, then danced in a circle. Later they had races. Soon the girls wanted to be pushed on the swings again.

Roxie shoved dead plants into a black garbage

bag. She carefully raked the dirt until it was smooth, then planted the few daffodil bulbs Mrs. Graham had instructed her to plant when she'd stopped by yesterday. When she was finished with that flower bed, she started on the other one. It was smaller and wouldn't take much time at all. She hurried as fast as she could just to get away from Stacia.

Just as Stacia was ready to take the girls inside, Hannah walked into the backyard. Her hair hung in two braids down her slender shoulders and flowed over her red jacket.

"Hannah!" the little girls cried together as they ran to hug her.

After the greetings, Hannah called Roxie over. "Did you girls hear that the Robbinses' garage windows were broken—just like your grandpa's were, Stacia."

"Heather Robbins told me on the bus," Roxie said.

Stacia only shrugged.

"It's really strange that two garages were vandalized on the same evening. That hasn't happened before last night." Hannah frowned thoughtfully as she pushed her hands into the pockets of her jacket.

Stacia swallowed hard. She decided to tell Hannah what she'd seen last night. "Last night after I left your house I saw someone with a flashlight outside the Robbinses' garage."

"No!" Hannah's face shone with excitement. "Tell me everything! Every single detail!"

"It's not much." Stacia told what she'd seen as quickly as she could.

"What about *your* garage?" Roxie asked.

Stacia stiffened. Did Roxie know something? "What about it?"

"Did you see the window broken?"

"Was it broken when you got back?" Hannah asked before Stacia could answer Roxie's question.

"I saw it was before I went in the house." Stacia almost choked on the words. At least she hadn't added lying to her sins.

"Then we know approximately the time the crimes were committed!" Hannah's eyes sparkled. "Now we're getting somewhere!"

Stacia trembled. What if Hannah learned the truth? Stacia took Kendall's and Rochelle's hands. "We have to go inside now. Bye." Stacia managed to smile at Hannah and Roxie.

The smile caught Roxie off-guard, and she smiled back.

Hannah said, "Be sure to get the first part of the report to me for our social studies special assignment."

Stacia nodded and hurried the little girls into the house. She really should find out what the assignment was. She frowned. Why should she? She wasn't going to do it anyway. She thought about

Hannah, and guilt flooded her. Abruptly she pushed the guilt away and helped the girls take off their jackets.

■

Outdoors Roxie finished the flower beds, dropped the plastic bag in the trash, and closed the garage door. She glanced at the house. She really wanted a drink of icy cold water, but no way would she go inside while Stacia was there.

Roxie brushed dirt off her hands as she hurried toward her own house. Pleasantly cool wind blew against her. Colored leaves fluttered to the ground, adding to the piles already there. She glanced at the street, and her heart stopped, then leaped wildly. Roy Marks was riding his bike toward her. Had he come to see her? Kathy lived outside the Ravines, so he wasn't here to see her.

Roy wheeled up on the sidewalk and slipped off his bike. "Hi, Roxie."

"Hi." Was her hair a mess? Did she have dirt on her cheeks as well as her hands?

"You said you'd show me your mom's carvings sometime. Can you now?"

"Sure." Roxie's eyes sparkled. She'd never dreamed Roy would actually come to her house. She glanced at her watch to see how much time she had before the Best Friends were to meet at Chelsea's. She had another half hour. And if Roy stayed longer, she'd just go to the meeting late. They'd understand.

Her heart sank. Kathy wouldn't. She'd be really mad.

Roxie smiled at Roy as they walked down the sidewalk. So what if Kathy got mad? She had no right.

"How are you coming on your social studies assignment?" Roy asked.

"I haven't started yet. Have you?"

"George and I are working together. He had an idea to do something about the Presidents, but I wanted to do something to show our area—like maybe artists and musicians and writers. Actors too, if there are any."

Roxie's heart sank. "So that's why you want to see Mom's work?"

Roy nodded. "And your grandpa's too, if I could."

"You can. We have a few pieces at my house, but Grandma lives on our street, so we can see what she has too."

"I thought I'd get a picture of the artist doing his work, then write a report about the arts in our own community." Roy stopped and studied Roxie. "You won't take my idea, will you?"

"Of course not!"

He sighed in relief. "I told George we should keep it a secret, but you're so easy to talk to, I forgot."

Roxie swelled with pride. She was easy to talk

to! He liked her! Maybe soon he'd like her more than he liked Kathy.

■

Several houses away Hannah stood outside the Robbinses' garage and studied the ground and the broken window. Stacia had seen someone with a flashlight prowling around the garage; then a few minutes later when she got home she found her garage window broken. Was the same culprit guilty? If so, he'd have had to run fast to get to her house to break the window. Stacia's grandma had said the window hadn't been broken just after dark. It had to have been broken between the time Stacia left and when she returned. Maybe the culprit had seen Stacia go back home.

Heather Robbins ran out her back door and stopped beside Hannah. "Did you come to baby-sit me?"

"No. I'm looking at the broken window."

"It's awful. My dad was really mad."

"If I knew who was vandalizing the area I'd stop him."

"Did you see Roxie today?" Heather asked.

"Yes. A while ago. She was cleaning the garden for Mrs. Graham."

"I want my mom to hire Roxie again. I just love her carvings. I wish she was my sister. Do you ever wish that?"

"I already have three sisters. But Roxie is one

of my best friends." Hannah glanced at her watch. "We have a meeting in a few minutes at Chelsea's house."

"Can I come?"

"Sorry. It's only for the four Best Friends."

"I wish I had a best friend."

"Start a Best Friends Club, Heather. Ask one or two or three girls your age to join it. Have talks, share a Scripture from the Bible, list things you can do to help others, and pray and play together. We even have sleepovers. It's really fun."

"I'll ask Mom if she knows a best friend for me." Heather hugged Hannah and ran to the house.

Smiling, Hannah looked at the ground again just in case there was a footprint or some other clue she'd missed.

■

Several blocks away Kathy rode her bike onto the shady street of The Ravines. How she longed to live there near the other Best Friends, but Mom and Dad said they'd never live in a house that looked exactly like all the others except for the color.

Kathy rode to Chelsea's yard and left her bike leaning against the garage. Suddenly she froze. Roy was just leaving Roxie's yard! Did he like Roxie instead of her? She'd expected him to continue to like her even though she liked Ty. Had Roxie told him she liked Ty better? Kathy pressed against the garage so Roy couldn't see her. She frowned. Why hide from him? She had no reason to hide from Roy Marks, a boy she'd known all her life. She ran into the open and called, "Hi, Roy!"

He glanced over and saw her and smiled happily. He wheeled up beside Kathy and slipped off his bike. "Hi! I didn't know you'd be in the neighborhood."

"We have a Best Friends meeting at Chelsea's."

"Can I join?" Roy laughed. "Just kidding."

Kathy locked her fingers together. "Were you visiting Roxie?"

"No. I'm doing a special assignment, and I had to talk to her mom."

Roxie was hidden behind a bush in her yard and heard Roy and Kathy. Roxie's heart dropped to her feet. Tears filled her eyes. Roy didn't like her at all! She'd been fooling herself into thinking he did. Anger at Kathy rushed through her, and it took all of her willpower to keep from confronting her even with Roy there.

After a million years Roy and Kathy said goodbye. Roy rode away, and Kathy ran to Chelsea's door. Roxie took a deep breath and finally walked to Chelsea's yard just as Hannah ran across the street.

"Hi, Roxie." Hannah flipped back her braids. "I've been thinking about asking Stacia to join the Best Friends."

"No! No way, Hannah!"

"Okay, okay—don't get so upset." Frowning, Hannah shook her head. "I don't know why you don't like her."

"She's so stuck on herself she doesn't think about anyone else."

Hannah shook her head. "She's upset that she can't live at home. That's all it is."

Roxie wanted to argue more but didn't. Hannah was wrong about Stacia, and she'd know soon enough.

A few minutes later the Best Friends sat in a circle on the floor in Chelsea's rec room. Mike had been playing Nintendo but had left so they could have their meeting. He'd wanted to show them his gymnastics, but Chelsea had refused to let him stay. She'd said little brothers were a major pain.

Roxie had wanted Mike to stay just so they couldn't start their meeting. It was hard to be in the same room with Kathy.

Chelsea rested her hands on her crossed legs. "Best Friends Club is now called to order. Hannah, did we do the good deed we said we'd do?"

"Yes. We took the Larson kids to the park so their mom could rest." Hannah glanced at the others. "For this week I'd like us to help Mrs. Prowess with her yard work. She doesn't have anyone to help her, and she doesn't have the money to pay anyone, Dad said."

"Who votes we help Mrs. Prowess?" Chelsea asked.

They all lifted their hands.

Chelsea turned to Kathy. "Do you have the Bible verse for today?"

"Me?" Kathy flushed. "I forgot!"

Chelsea shook her head. "I'm surprised. You usually remember. Does anyone else have a verse?"

Roxie bit her lower lip. She hadn't read her Bible for the past five days. She couldn't even remember a single verse to quote.

Hannah took a deep breath. "The only one I can think of right now is one Dad read this morning. It's about strife." Hannah frowned in thought. "'Where there is strife there is every evil work.'" She shrugged. "Or something like that. He said strife is one of Satan's biggest weapons. If he can get Christians to be upset and fighting with each other, it leaves them wide open for him to bring in other evil works."

"That's terrible!" Chelsea shivered. "I read that verse before, but I'd forgotten about it. If we're in strife but pretend we're not, it still gives Satan an opening to bring in more trouble for us."

Roxie and Kathy glanced at each other and quickly looked away.

"I'd like us to pray for Stacia King," Hannah said. "She's very upset that she can't live at home."

"You lead in prayer." Chelsea took Roxie's

hand, then Kathy's. "Should we pray for anyone else?"

The others shrugged, so Hannah prayed for Stacia. Roxie bit her lip. It was hard to sit still and listen to Hannah.

Later Chelsea flipped on her stomach and said, "I saw a sweater at the mall that I want so much!"

Hannah laughed. "You always see something you want." She sighed heavily. "I wish we could find a way to help Stacia King move back home. But it would take more money than we could raise."

"Stop talking about Stacia King," Roxie snapped.

The others looked at her, and she flushed crimson red.

"Okay, so I'm sorry." Roxie folded her arms and scowled.

"You'd better settle your feelings about Stacia or you'll really be sorry," Chelsea said in her Oklahoma accent.

"Why don't you learn to talk right?" Roxie jabbed Chelsea's arm. "We get tired of hearing you say your words so funny."

Chelsea's eyes widened. "But *you're* the ones who talk wrong! How can you say *I* do?"

Kathy patted Chelsea's leg. "Don't mind Roxie. Everything makes her mad these days."

"Especially the way you flirt with Ty and still try to keep Roy as a boyfriend!" Roxie jumped up.

"I'm going home. I might not come to the next Best Friends meeting—especially if Kathy's here."

Kathy flushed. "See who cares, Roxie! Stay away all you want."

Hannah helplessly shook her head. "Please don't fight, girls. We're Best Friends, remember?"

Roxie ran up the stairs and slammed the door. She was tired of pretending to be friends with Kathy. Maybe she'd even stop being friends with Chelsea from dumb old Oklahoma and Hannah, the Ottawa Indian.

9

Black Stacia

The sun shone down on Roxie as she looked at a blister on the inside of her thumb, frowned, then picked up the rake again. Mrs. Prowess's yard was huge! Roxie raked more colored leaves onto the pile. Why did she ever vote to rake it for free, especially on a Friday afternoon when there was no school? Sometimes she was so nice it made her sick.

Across the yard Kathy, Chelsea, and Hannah were talking and laughing as they worked. They seemed to be having fun, but Kathy was only pretending. Ty had asked her to meet him at the mall, and she had agreed. She wasn't supposed to, and she knew it, but she just couldn't turn him down. He had asked her to hang out at the mall! What a wonderful way to spend a Friday afternoon! She wanted to tell the Best Friends, but she knew they would try to talk her out of going. And she was going! Nothing could stop her. Nothing!

Just then Stacia walked past on the sidewalk with Heather Robbins running along beside her. Heather stopped when she saw Roxie.

"Roxie!" Heather shouted joyfully, then ran across the yard to her. "How come you didn't baby-sit me today?"

"I already had this job." Roxie motioned to the yard with a swish of her leaf rake. "Or I would have."

Stacia hesitated, then walked over to Hannah, Kathy, and Chelsea to talk to them.

Heather watched the girls talking, then looked up at Roxie. "Why don't you like Stacia?"

Roxie forced back a cry of dismay. "I didn't say I didn't."

"You didn't talk to her or smile at her."

"I'm busy."

Heather narrowed her eyes and pursed her lips. "You always smile at me and talk to me even when you're busy."

Roxie's heart sank. Why was Heather so observant?

Heather looked across the yard at Stacia as she laughed at something Chelsea had said. Heather turned back to Roxie and whispered, "Did you know Stacia is black?"

"Of course."

Heather studied Roxie. "Is that why you don't like her?"

Roxie frowned. "I don't want to talk about it."

Heather flipped her hair back. "I don't like Stacia either. She's black, and I don't like her."

Roxie's stomach tightened. "Stop it, Heather! I didn't say anything against her for being black."

Heather flipped back her hair again and looked smug. "You want me to like her because that's what Jesus wants. But I'm like you, Roxie. I carve animals like you. And I'm going to be a *King's Kid* like you when I'm old enough. And, like you, I don't like Stacia at all."

Roxie bit back a groan. Why would Heather copy *her*? She wasn't a good role model. She frantically searched for the right words. "I want you to like Stacia. She's your baby-sitter for this afternoon."

"I want *you* to watch me, Roxie!"

"I already have a job."

"But we have so much fun together."

"Sorry."

Heather dashed across the lawn shouting, "Stacia, you're black and we don't like you. Me and Roxie don't!"

Stacia's face burned. How dare Roxie turn Heather against her!

Roxie ran after Heather and grabbed her by the arm. "Stop it!"

Heather looked wide-eyed at Roxie. "What's wrong? Why are you mad at me?"

Helplessly Roxie shook her head. What could she say? Heather was right—she didn't like Stacia. It didn't have anything to do with her being black, but Heather would never believe that. Heather could be very stubborn. "I'm not mad at you. I want you to go with Stacia like you're supposed to and be a good girl."

Heather crossed her arms and stuck out her chin. "No! I won't go with Black Stacia! I mean it. I'm going to stay with you. You can baby-sit me."

"But I can't! Stacia will do it."

Stacia forced back scalding tears as she turned to Chelsea. "Give Roxie the job. I'll switch with her. She can baby-sit Heather and I'll rake."

Roxie wanted to sink out of sight.

"This is our good deed," Hannah said, waving her arm to take in the whole yard. "We don't get paid for it."

Stacia's heart sank. She desperately needed the money. She looked at Heather and knew it wouldn't do any good to try to take her back home. Stacia stared at Roxie. *She* was to blame. She'd made Heather hate her! Stacia faced Chelsea. "I'll change jobs anyway. You can see Heather wants to be with Roxie."

Roxie bit back an argument. Heather was used to getting her own way. Roxie knew that no matter what she said, Heather wouldn't go with Stacia.

Chelsea sighed and nodded. She knew Heather

well. She was usually a sweet little girl, but she could be very, very stubborn. "I'll explain to Mrs. Robbins. She won't mind Roxie taking over." Chelsea turned to Roxie. "You'll take care of Heather, won't you?"

Roxie nodded. What else could she do?

"I'm glad," Heather said with a smug look. "We don't want to be around Black Stacia."

"Heather!" Roxie grabbed Heather's arm and dragged her away.

"I'm sorry," Hannah said softly.

"It's not your fault." Stacia picked up Roxie's rake and raked hard and fast. The taunting words "Black Stacia" rang inside her head, and she raked even harder.

Kathy moved restlessly. She had to get home to shower and change so she could meet Ty at the mall. "I have to go home now, Chel. Sorry I can't help finish."

"How come?" Hannah asked.

Kathy brushed back her blonde curls. "I have an errand to run."

"I guess we can finish without you." Chelsea watched Kathy run to her bike and ride away. "I wonder what she's going to do."

"I don't know." Hannah sighed. "I wish she and Roxie would make up."

"They will. We've been praying for them."

Hannah smiled and nodded.

Stacia bit her lower lip. It would be nice to belong to the Best Friends—to play and pray and work together. Abruptly she pushed the thought aside. She wouldn't live here long enough to become a Best Friend, so why even think about it?

■

At the crowded mall Kathy looked at her reflection in the Gantos window. Her blonde curls framed her face and touched her pink sweater. She'd used her mom's lip gloss and looked at least fourteen. She tried to smile but couldn't. She was excited about seeing Ty, but she felt really really bad about sneaking off to meet him. The usual sounds of the mall seemed extra-loud.

Finally she spotted Ty at a table at the cookie store. He was eating a big cookie and drinking a glass of pop. Her hands turned icy cold even as her heart leaped. She almost turned and ran back outdoors to her bike, then squared her shoulders and walked around the flow of traffic to the table. The smell of cookies drifted to her. "Hi." She sounded as if she'd run all the way from her house.

"Hi ya, Kathy." Ty motioned to a chair. A strand of blond hair fell across his forehead. His blue eyes crinkled as he smiled. "Sit down. Want a bite of my cookie?"

"Sure. Thanks." What else could she say?

He broke off a bite and handed it to her. She ate it but couldn't taste a thing.

Ty leaned forward. "Bring any money?"

Kathy stiffened. "A little."

"I thought we could play some video games, but I have to save my money for a movie later."

Kathy hesitated, then pulled a couple of dollars from the pocket of her jeans.

Ty snatched it up. "Thanks. Come on."

Slowly Kathy stood, then hurried after him. He walked so fast she had to run to catch up. She saw a green and yellow sweater in a store window, but she couldn't stop to look at it without Ty losing her in the crowd.

In the arcade Ty stuck money in the slot, and immediately the game began.

Kathy stood beside him and tried to act excited every time he blew up an airplane. He forgot she was even there. She stood on one foot, then another. He racked up thousands of points, his eyes glued to the screen. The noise of the games seemed extra-loud. Boys and girls at the other games cried with joy when they won and with anger when they lost. Ty's game finally ended, and she started to step over to take her turn, but he stayed where he was, his face intent, his shoulders hunched.

With a weary sigh Kathy walked to the doorway and leaned against the door frame. Would Ty even notice if she left?

"Kathy!"

She turned and saw Roy. She smiled in relief. "Hi! Are you alone?"

He nodded. "Mom sent me to get socks for my little brother." Roy made a face. "Socks! Who said hanging out at the mall was fun?"

Kathy giggled. She'd lots rather be shopping for socks with Roy than waiting for Ty to finish a boring video game.

"Are you alone?" Roy looked past her and saw Ty. Roy's face fell. "I guess not."

"Actually, I am alone. I thought I was with Ty, but he's so caught up with his game he doesn't notice I'm around."

"Want to go with me to find socks for Ben? White tube socks. No colored band at the top. All cotton."

Kathy giggled again. She looked over her shoulder at Ty. "I'll tell him I'm going. I'll be right back." She hurried to Ty and tried to wait until she was sure he heard her. Finally she blurted out, "I'm leaving now."

He didn't look at her or say a word.

"Bye," she said with a sigh. She walked back to Roy. "I'm ready."

"Good. I hate shopping alone. Especially for something as important as white tube socks for Ben." Roy laughed.

Smiling happily, Kathy fell into step beside him.

■

In the Robbinses' kitchen Roxie set a glass of milk and a plate of chocolate-chip cookies in front of Heather, then sat beside her. Sunshine fell across the potted plant blooming with white flowers. "After our snack we'll go to the park a while."

"Good! I like the park." Heather drank deeply, then set her glass down. A milk mustache covered her upper lip. Roxie handed her a napkin, and she wiped it off.

Roxie leaned back in her chair. "Heather, I want you to like Stacia. She really is okay."

Heather picked up a cookie but didn't bite into it. She studied Roxie thoughtfully. "Then why don't you like her?"

Roxie shrugged helplessly. Why didn't she like Stacia? She remembered the night she'd met her. "She made fun of my art."

"Kids at my school made fun of my purple pig. I guess I'll quit liking them."

Roxie frowned. "You know that isn't right."

"What's right for you is right for me." Heather took a large bite of cookie.

Roxie hung her head. How could she make such a mess of things? "Heather, you can't always copy me!"

"Sure, I can. I love you, and I want to be just like you."

Roxie groaned as she frantically searched for the right words. But would words help?

Hannah, Chelsea, and Stacia piled the last leaf bag in the cart at the curb for the trash man to pick up just as Mrs. Prowess walked out her door. She was older than Stacia's grandma and walked with a cane.

"Girls, the yard looks beautiful! How can I begin to thank you enough?"

Hannah smiled. "You've already thanked us enough." She had thanked them about five times already.

Mrs. Prowess brushed tears from her eyes. "I never met anyone before who'd help me without charging me. You know I'd pay if I could."

"We wouldn't take the money," Chelsea said, smiling. "We voted ahead of time to do this as a good deed. We like helping others."

Stacia hung back a little. She'd never on purpose done a good deed for a stranger. It felt good.

"Could you girls come inside? I want to give you something."

Hannah shook her head. "We won't take pay."

"It's not pay. It's my way of saying thank you." Mrs. Prowess brushed a strand of white hair off her wrinkled cheek. The legs of her black pants flapped around her thin legs as she walked unsteadily back inside.

The girls looked questioningly at each other, shrugged, and followed Mrs. Prowess. Her house was immaculate and smelled like apple and cinnamon potpourri. Piano music from the radio played softly in the background.

Mrs. Prowess picked up a wooden bowl. "Years ago I collected Petoskey stones when my husband and I went up north. I want you girls to have one each."

Chelsea frowned. "What's a Petoskey stone?"

Hannah handed her one. "See the special markings on it—gray circles with funny white and gray lines around them? The stones are found only in a few places and are used for jewelry or decoration."

Chelsea studied the smooth stone. "I never saw anything like it in my whole life! It's almost like tiny lacy doilies imbedded in it. Even on the bottom!"

"It's very unique." Mrs. Prowess picked up a stone and rubbed it. "I hope you girls treasure the stones as much as I do."

"Thank you," Stacia said softly. "My grandpa has several, and I always wanted one. Now I have my own." She pushed it into the front pocket of her jeans. When she got home—*her* home, not her grandparents'—she'd show her little sisters. She'd even let them touch it any time they wanted.

Later Stacia walked slowly down to Grandpa's studio. He was still at work, and Grandma was taking a nap. "I'll only sing for a little while," she whispered as she gently closed the soundproof door.

Shivering with a little fear and a lot of excitement, Stacia picked up the cassette of her song. She clicked on the mike and smiled.

Stacia's Song

In the studio Stacia stood tall, lifted her chin, and reached for a high note. She hit it without a flaw, her voice flowing out better than she'd ever heard it. Shivers tingled over her body, and tears pricked her eyes. She was a singer! Maybe she really could be another Stacia Robedioux! Maybe someday crowds would be shouting for Stacia King. They wouldn't make fun of her and call her "Black Stacia." They'd be glad she was black.

After a long time the last note faded away. Stacia stood very still, hearing the song in her head and feeling it in her heart.

"Stacia King!"

Her spine tingling, she spun around and came face to face with Grandpa. He sounded angry, but tears stood in his eyes. He took a step toward her. She shrieked and ran past him up the stairs.

"Stacia!" he roared.

Breathing hard, she stopped in the kitchen where Grandma was filling a blue plastic ice cube tray with water.

"What on earth?" Grandma dropped the tray in the sink and caught Stacia's hand. "What's wrong? You look like you saw a ghost."

"I didn't mean to do anything wrong," Stacia said hoarsely. "I was singing in Grandpa's studio, and he caught me there. I think he's going to beat me."

"Don't be ridiculous." Grandma pushed Stacia onto a chair and gave her a glass of water. "Take a drink and calm down. Grandpa was probably angry that you were in his studio, but he'd never lay a finger on you. You know that."

Stacia sighed in relief. She drank half a glass of water and felt better. "I only wanted to sing."

"Grandpa's not used to sharing his studio, what with your Uncle Anthony gone on tour. I'm sure he won't care if you use it as long as you're careful and don't ruin anything."

Stacia nodded, but she was sure she'd never have the courage to go into the studio again. Grandpa had definitely been angry—so angry he'd cried. She did that herself sometimes.

Just then something Grandma said caught Stacia's attention. They'd never talked about Uncle Anthony. Maybe this was a perfect time to ask about him. "What kind of tour is Uncle Anthony on?"

Grandma glanced toward the door. She said in a low voice, "You know he's a singer."

But Stacia didn't know. If anyone had ever said that, she hadn't been listening.

Again Grandma looked toward the door. "He's the road man for Leroy Drake, who sings gospel and rhythm and blues."

"What's wrong with that?"

"Anthony's got such talent and voice, he could be the musician, not just the roady. But he's afraid to try to have his own career. That hurts Grandpa a lot. So don't talk to him about Anthony."

Stacia shrugged. She wasn't about to talk to Grandpa about *anything*.

Grandma brushed at Stacia's jeans. "Look at that dirt! Get them off and I'll wash them so they'll be clean for tomorrow."

"I can do it myself at home, Grandma."

"I know, but I have a load ready to start. Take your jeans off and toss them down to me."

Stacia ran upstairs before she made Grandma as mad as she'd made Grandpa. She pulled off her jeans and tossed them downstairs where Grandma was waiting for them. Stacia slipped on another pair of jeans and ran back downstairs. She'd help Grandma fix supper. She didn't want Grandma to give a bad report to Mom and Dad when they came in the morning. Stacia thought about the garage window Grandpa had had to replace. She flushed. Maybe she should tell the truth. But then she thought about Grandpa's anger and shook her head. It was better if he never learned she'd broken the window—especially since she'd done it on purpose.

"Stacia!" Grandma stepped into the kitchen from the laundry room. Her eyes were flashing, and she held something in her hand. "How could you steal from Grandpa?"

With a strangled cry Stacia fell back a step and bumped right into Grandpa.

"What did she steal?" Grandpa's voice was gruffer than usual.

"This!" Grandma laid the Petoskey stone on the table. "How could you, Stacia? You know never to touch his collection."

"I knew this wouldn't work," Grandpa said, raking his hand across his face.

Stacia stared at them and helplessly shook her head. "It's *my* stone! I didn't steal it!"

"Now, Stacia, where would you get a Petoskey stone?" Grandma held it out to Grandpa, but he didn't take it. "Apologize to your grandpa right this instant."

"No . . . No!" Stacia balled her fists. "It *is* my stone! I got it today. Why don't you believe me?"

Grandma's face hardened. "You were baby-sitting Heather Robbins today. How could you get the stone then?"

"But I wasn't baby-sitting! I changed jobs with Roxie Shoulders. I raked leaves for Mrs. Prowess. She gave each of us a stone."

"Don't lie," Grandpa snapped. "That old woman wouldn't give away anything."

"But she did!" Stacia leaned weakly back against the kitchen counter. "Call Chelsea McCrea if you don't believe me. Or Hannah Shigwam. They got stones too."

Grandpa impatiently waved his hand. "Give her the stone back, Parleen. She must be telling the truth."

Stacia's mouth dropped open in shock. Grandpa believed her!

Grandma slowly handed the stone to Stacia. "I'm sorry. I guess I should've known you wouldn't steal or do anything else bad."

Burning with shame at breaking the garage window, Stacia took the stone and dropped it in her pocket. Maybe it would be wiser to give it to Grandpa. It might make him less grumpy. But she left it in her pocket.

Grandpa cleared his throat. "Stacia, you can use my studio as long as you do it when I'm not home. Just you be careful not to break anything, you hear?"

Stacia barely nodded. She'd heard, but she

couldn't believe she'd heard right. He wouldn't really allow her to use the studio, would he? She studied him to see if he'd take it back, but he didn't.

"Don't strain so hard to reach the high notes. You got 'em in you, so let 'em out." Grandpa turned away and filled a glass with water, then drained it dry.

Stacia looked from Grandpa to Grandma.

"We'll have supper ready soon." Grandma smiled hesitantly. "Arnold, you have time to practice if you want."

Grandpa walked out of the kitchen without another word.

Stacia fingered the stone in her pocket. Maybe after tomorrow she wouldn't be around to use Grandpa's studio. Mom and Dad just might agree to take her back home. Her heart fluttered. But what if they didn't?

■

At the park Roxie pushed Heather high on the swing. They'd already been there an hour, and it was time to go home. Heather wanted to stay longer. She liked getting her own way. Usually Roxie knew how to make her obey.

"How come Stacia's black?" Heather asked over her shoulder as she swung forward, her feet straight out in front, her long hair streaming out behind her.

Roxie frowned. What had she created? Heather

had always accepted people the way they were without noticing anyone was different from anyone else. Roxie took a deep breath before she answered, "She's black because God made her that way."

"Like He made us white and He made Hannah an Ottawa Indian?"

"That's right."

"So Stacia can't help it that she's black?"

"No. She's glad she is."

"Not us, though. We don't want her to be black. We don't like her."

Roxie caught the swing and jerked it to a stop. "I told you not to say that again! Jesus said to love everyone, didn't He?"

Heather hung her head and whispered, "Yes."

Roxie could barely get the words past the lump in her throat. "And we have to obey Him, right?"

Heather nodded.

"So what are we going to do?"

"Love Stacia."

"That's right." Roxie crossed her fingers behind her back. *She* wasn't going to love Stacia, but Heather was.

Heather jumped off the swing. "I guess we better go tell Stacia."

Roxie froze. How could she do that? "Let's tell her later. You have to get back home now."

Thoughtfully Heather looked up at Roxie.

"Are we going to change our minds and hate her again?"

Roxie flushed. "No . . . No, we're not."

Heather grinned. "Good. It doesn't feel good to hate anyone."

Roxie nodded. Heather was right—it didn't feel good at all.

■

Kathy stood her bike in the stand inside the garage beside Duke's and Brody's, then turned to Roy. "Thanks for riding home with me."

Roy shrugged and grinned. "It was fun, wasn't it?"

Kathy nodded. "I'm really sorry I went with Ty. I guess he's addicted to arcade games."

Roy rolled his eyes. "I guess."

Kathy and Roy walked around back and sat on the picnic table. Guitar music drifted out from the music room. Duke and Brody were practicing as usual. Megan's sandbox was full of leaves. Kathy sighed. They'd raked leaves up about a hundred times already. How many times would they have to do it before all the leaves were gone?

"Do you have to rake leaves, Roy?"

"Sure. I get tired of it. How about you?"

"I hate it! When I grow up I'll never rake another leaf! I mean it."

"I guess I'd rather rake leaves than live in the city where I might not have a tree in my yard."

"I wonder where I'll live? Maybe in the South where the winters aren't so cold."

"Not me! I like ice fishing, ice skating, skiing. I like winter."

They talked about school and church and what they wanted to do during Christmas vacation even though it was two months away.

Suddenly Ty Wilton stepped around the house and said gruffly, "Where'd you go, Kathy? I turned around to talk to you in the arcade and you were gone!"

Kathy's face flamed. "I told you I was leaving."

Roy jumped off the table. "Get out of here, Wilton. We don't want you around."

His hair damp with perspiration, Ty walked to Kathy's side. "You don't want me to leave, do you?" He smiled his best smile.

Kathy's bones melted, and she returned his smile. "I'm glad you came."

Roy sputtered angrily.

Kathy turned to Roy. "I'm sure you don't want to stay while I talk with Ty, do you?"

Roy swallowed hard. "I guess not." He ran to his bike and pedaled away.

Kathy patted the picnic table. "Sit down, Ty."

"I thought we were going to a movie."

"It's too late now. I have to help make dinner in a few minutes."

Ty glanced at his watch, then jumped up beside

Kathy. "I got my highest score yet on the game. I thought you'd stay beside me and see how good I was."

"It was a little boring, Ty."

"It was?" Ty shrugged. "I thought you liked arcade games."

"I do, but I like it when I can have a turn."

"I didn't think of that. Next time, huh?" Ty smiled and moved closer to her.

She nodded. She searched her mind for something to say. "Want to listen to my brothers play their guitars?"

Ty shook his head. "I'm not into their kind of music."

"Oh."

He talked about the music he liked—songs that she never listened to because of the kinds of activities they sang about.

As soon as she could, she changed the subject to pets. "I always wanted a dog."

"I have one. Rusty. He's a spaniel, and I trained him myself." Ty's face glowed as he talked about his dog. "I have a part-time job cleaning the cages at the animal shelter."

"That's nice."

He shrugged. "I like it. It makes me feel bad when they have to put some of them to sleep though." He told about several of the dogs and cats that he'd especially liked that had been adopted by someone.

Kathy moved restlessly. She hadn't realized Ty talked so much. He never let her say more than a word or two. Roy wasn't like that. They talked about the same. Ty didn't seem to notice that he was monopolizing the conversation.

Finally he jumped to the ground. "I've got to go, Kathy. See you Monday in school."

"See you." She walked to his bike with him and watched him pedal away. She stood a long time adjusting to the silence. With a deep sigh she walked inside. Maybe she'd talk to him in the hall Monday between classes. She smiled dreamily.

Did he always do all the talking when they were together? She thought about it and nodded. Her smile wavered.

■

Hannah stood outside Stacia's grandparents' home and looked at the rock Mrs. Smith said had been used to break the window. Now it was back in the flower bed where it belonged. "Something's wrong," Hannah muttered as she tapped her chin with her fingertip. All the other windows had been broken with a club of some kind. Why was this one broken with a rock?

Just then Stacia walked out the front door and ran across the yard to join Hannah. "Are you looking for clues?"

"Yes." Hannah told her what she'd been thinking. "So I wonder if someone else broke this window."

Stacia's skin pricked with guilt and fear. Hannah was a little too smart.

Before Hannah could speak again, Heather ran up to Stacia.

"I'm sorry for being mean to you, Stacia. Jesus says to love you, so I do. I like you black. You can baby-sit me anytime you want and I'll be nice to you."

"Thank you." Stacia didn't know what else to say.

"Roxie said we have to obey Jesus," Heather said with a smile. "I'm glad I don't hate you any longer because I do like you."

"Thank you." Stacia looked helplessly at Hannah.

"We're glad you came to apologize to Stacia." Hannah hugged Heather. "You're a nice girl. I think you'd like my sisters and they'd like you."

"I forgot all about them! I've been praying for best friends. You think I could go see them right now?"

Hannah nodded. "Ask your mom first though."

Heather ran off, her hair whipping around her thin shoulders.

"Lena has been praying for a best friend,"

Hannah said softly. "I think her prayer was just answered."

"God does answer prayer, doesn't He?" Stacia took a deep breath. "I've been praying I can live at home again."

"Your mom and dad must not think it's the best for you or they wouldn't have brought you here."

"But home *is* the best for me!" Stacia bit her lip. "Even though the school really isn't all that good. And it is scary to walk back and forth."

"Maybe you should pray that your parents will find a house in an area where the school is better."

"But I want to go home now!"

"Even if it's not safe?"

Stacia whirled around and ran to the house.

Hannah sighed heavily. Slowly she walked back home, silently praying for Stacia.

■

Saturday morning Stacia woke up with a start. Today Mom and Dad were coming! She jumped out of bed and pulled her suitcase out of the closet. She'd get ready for them to take her home. But what if they didn't? The corners of her mouth turned down, and slowly she pushed the suitcase back into the closet. If they decided to take her home, she'd pack then.

She pulled on clean jeans and an orange and yellow sweater. She used her red pick on her hair and held her hair back with a wide yellow ponytail band. She should've told Hannah good-bye yesterday just in case.

"She'll forget about me anyway, so why bother?"

Slowly Stacia walked downstairs. The smell of bacon and toast filled the house but didn't make her feel hungry. She was too tense to eat. But she knew Grandma would make her eat anyway. Grandma said it wasn't healthy to go without breakfast.

Stacia started to walk into the kitchen but stopped when she heard Grandpa mention her name. Her insides fluttered. She had to know what Grandpa was saying about her.

"That girl's got a voice, Parleen. Bethany's got to see she gets voice lessons."

"It'll never happen where they live now."

"Then we'll look around here and find a teacher for her."

Stacia pressed her hand to her racing heart. Voice lessons! She'd wanted them since she was five years old! She shook her head. She didn't like what she was thinking. She wouldn't stay here even to take voice lessons!

She took a deep breath and walked into the kitchen. "Morning. I think I'll just have toast today."

Grandma shook her head. "You'll do no such thing. You're having bacon, eggs, toast, and a glass of milk. How can a growing girl get energy without a good breakfast?"

Stacia popped in two pieces of whole wheat toast while Grandma broke two eggs into a skillet. Grandpa drank his coffee without saying a word. He didn't even look at Stacia. Had she heard him correctly? Had he really talked about her and her voice? Maybe she'd imagined it all. She peeked at him from under her black lashes. He never looked up and he never said another word all the time she sat in the kitchen eating the breakfast she really didn't want.

She glanced at her watch. It was already nine o'clock. What if her family didn't come? Her stomach tightened, and she pushed away from the table.

11

Stacia's Family

With butterflies fluttering in her stomach, Stacia sat on the porch and waited for her family. The sun was summer-bright and almost summer-warm. The smell of baking bread drifted out of an open window behind her. Grandma knew they all liked homemade bread. Grandpa was in his studio and had said not to bother him until the family got there. Stacia sat on her hands, then pulled them out and laced her fingers together. It was sooo hard to wait!

A blue station wagon drove down the street, and Stacia leaped to her feet. The car drove past, and Stacia sank back down. Across the street a dog barked. Stacia watched the dog run around a house. It soon stopped barking, perhaps when someone fed it.

Another blue station wagon pulled into the driveway and stopped outside the garage. It was her family!

With a wild shout, Stacia leaped off the porch and ran to the station wagon. Before she reached it, the three little girls were already out. They all hugged her at the same time, almost knocking her over. She laughed and cried and hugged them back; then she hugged Mom. Stacia wished she could stay in Mom's arms forever.

"When do I get a turn?" Dad's voice was rough with tears as he pulled Stacia close.

Stacia pressed her face against Dad's neck. She smelled his aftershave and felt the thud of his heart. She'd taken hugs and kisses from her family for granted, but never again. They just had to let her return with them! She couldn't survive if they didn't.

Grandma and Grandpa greeted everyone, then led them all inside while everyone talked at once—everyone but Grandpa. As usual he didn't say a word. He sat in his chair in the living room, while Grandma sat on the couch between Stacia's mom and dad. The little girls and Stacia sat on the soft carpet. The girls made sure they were touching Stacia. It was as if they couldn't get enough of her. And she couldn't get enough of being with them either. If she didn't get to return with them, she would shrivel up and die. "Families belong together"—Mom and Dad had both said that over as over as long as she could remember. But now they'd changed their minds. Stacia pressed her lips together. She was going to do everything in her power to change their minds back!

"How was school, Sta?" Mom asked, smiling warmly.

Stacia shrugged. "Different. Okay, I guess. But I'd rather be home and go to my own school, even if it is in a bad neighborhood." Oh, why had she said that? It would give them a chance to think of what to say when she said she was going home with them to stay.

"You're staying where you are," Dad said firmly.

Stacia wanted to argue but knew it was better to wait. "I did meet several kids, and I joined *King's Kids*." She told them about *King's Kids*, but not that she'd joined in order to make money so she could get home sooner.

"Lorraine said to say hi," Candace said.

Stacia forced a smile. "Tell her hi."

Ariel leaned her face against Stacia's. "Lorraine and Rana have been practicing together. But Lorraine said you're better than Rana."

"She sings like this." Tiffany sang a song and flatted half the notes, then giggled so hard she fell into Stacia's lap.

Mom picked up a throw pillow and held it in her lap. She wore blue slacks and a pink and blue sweater. "Have you heard from Anthony lately, Momma?"

Grandma looked quickly at Grandpa.

"Well, answer your daughter," he snapped. "Don't mind me. I won't fly into a rage from hearing somebody talk about my son."

Stacia shushed the little girls so she could hear Grandma's answer. Suddenly she wanted to know all she could about Uncle Anthony. Why hadn't she known he could sing and play piano?

Grandma moved restlessly in her chair. "I got a call a couple days ago. He might be in town this weekend."

Grandpa frowned.

Stacia thought he was going to say something, but he didn't. How in the world could he keep all those words locked inside? She'd never be able to do that. In fact, she often said things she later wished she hadn't said. Maybe Grandpa didn't say anything so he'd never have to feel sorry for saying the wrong thing.

"I hope he comes while we're here," Mom said.

Dad nodded. "It's been a year since we've seen him."

"Maybe we can sing together again." Mom laughed softly. "I used to daydream about going on the road—Smith and Smith. I had it all worked out. But I had to finish school, and then I got married."

Stacia stared at Mom in shock. She'd never heard Mom sing and was amazed to learn that Mom had dreamed about going on musical tours.

"I brought a Carman song with me that I'd love to sing with Anthony." Mom chuckled. "Carman has white skin, but he sure can sing like he's black!" She turned to Stacia. "We brought his new album for you, Sta."

She smiled. "Thanks." She liked his singing almost as much as Stacia Robedioux's.

Later Stacia walked upstairs alone. She hesitated outside Uncle Anthony's room. She'd never thought about looking inside before. Now she wanted to. She listened to the family downstairs. The little girls were outdoors in the yard with Dad, Grandpa was in his studio, and Mom and Grandma were in the kitchen making a picnic lunch to take to the park.

Stacia opened the door and looked inside. The room was almost bare, having only a bed without a spread and just one dresser. Why would Grandpa tell her to stay out of this room? There was nothing here worth looking at. But she stood there anyway, looking at Uncle Anthony's room and thinking about him. Why was he a roady for Leroy Drake when he had so much talent and training of his own?

Slowly Stacia closed the door. She turned, then gasped when she saw Uncle Anthony standing just down the hall watching her. He was younger than Mom by seven years. Right now he looked very sleepy. He wore pleated jeans and a white cotton shirt. His curls were clipped close to his head. He was the best-looking man she'd ever seen.

"See anything interesting in my room?" Anthony walked toward her, his black pack flung over his broad shoulder. His black western boots clicked loudly on the pine floor.

She felt on fire with embarrassment. "Sorry. I was . . . interested to know more about you."

"How come?"

"Because I sing too."

He flung his pack into his room. "Who's your favorite?"

"Stacia Robedioux."

Anthony chuckled as he hugged Stacia close. "Your namesake. I like her too. I was talking to her last week."

Stacia pulled away from Anthony and stared at him in awe. "Tell me every single word you said and she said."

"She wanted to know about me. I gave her one of my songs, and she said she'd listen to it and maybe use it on her next album."

"You have got to be kidding!" Stacia clasped her hands together. "This is too good to be true! Tell me about the song. I want to hear it."

"Let's go to the studio and I'll sing it for you. Pop hasn't heard it. He might not like it." Anthony rubbed a hand over his curls and sighed heavily. "Pop's really good. One of the best."

"Grandpa?"

Anthony nodded. "Haven't you heard his albums? He had three before he quit the business to stay home with the family."

"Three albums? I didn't know that!" She couldn't imagine Grandpa actually making albums and singing in front of crowds.

"Let's go." Anthony caught Stacia's hand and walked quickly to the stairs.

At the top of the basement steps Stacia pulled back. "Grandpa says I can't go to his studio when he's there. Only when he's not."

"Don't worry. He's in the kitchen with Momma and Bethany." Anthony held out his hand. "Come on."

Stacia took his hand and walked down to the studio. She could feel Anthony's excitement. She watched him as he snapped in the demo tape. He motioned for her to sit on the canvas director's chair, and he perched on the edge of the desk. She trembled. What if she didn't like the song?

Anthony's voice leaped out of the speakers and filled the studio. The song was about God's great love and the authority He's given to His people. Stacia knew the title without being told—"His Spirit in You."

Tears filled Stacia's eyes and trickled down her cheeks. She'd forgotten she was connected with God Himself and that He was her Heavenly Father.

When she'd gotten mad at Mom and Dad, she'd pulled away from God to get back at them. But *she'd* been the one who was hurt. She'd forgotten she could be victorious no matter what the situation or circumstances.

Anthony turned the demo over and played only the instrumental. He turned on the mike and sang his song. Hearing the song live was even better than on tape. He sang it through twice, then handed her a sheet with the words on it. "Sing with me."

Stacia's eyes widened. Shivers ran up and down her spine. She was going to sing an original song by her uncle that Stacia Robedioux might be putting on her next album!

Anthony nodded, and together they sang his song. She sang the lead, and he harmonized. The words touched her so deeply, she was covered with goose bumps.

When the song ended, a wonderful silence filled the studio. Anthony looked at Stacia with a strange expression on his face. He pulled her close and held her tight. "You have a gift, Stacia—a gift from God. Don't let anyone keep you from using that gift to touch others for Jesus."

"I won't," Stacia whispered. For the first time in a week she had something more important to think about than going home with her parents.

"So, I hear you're staying with Momma and Pop."

Stacia nodded.

"Because of the school you have to go to in Brazelton."

She shrugged. He wouldn't understand that they didn't want to bother with her since they had the little girls. The house was too small for all of them—too small and in the wrong part of town. The elementary school the little girls attended was less than a block from their house, so they didn't have any trouble getting there. Her school was too far away, and she had to go through a bad part of town to get there. All together it was a bother for her parents to keep her at home.

Anthony glanced at his watch. "We better get upstairs. My watch and my stomach say it's time to eat. We're having a picnic at the park."

"That'll be fun since you're here."

He hugged her, then followed her upstairs. He stopped her outside the kitchen and whispered, "Don't forget what I told you. Do all you can to train your voice, and sing whenever you can. Don't you let anybody or anything stop you from serving God with the talent He's given you!"

His words stayed with her while she sat at the picnic table in the park. Her family laughed and talked. Even Grandpa told a story about when he was a boy. Stacia couldn't imagine him being young. To her he'd always been old and crabby. As hard as she tried, she just couldn't imagine him on tour entertaining thousands of people.

After the food was packed away, Stacia's mom said, "Anthony, why don't you and I sing a few songs together. I came prepared."

Anthony darted a look at his dad, then laughed. "Shall we sing for our supper, Bethany? Just like in the old days."

She grinned and nodded.

Stacia watched her mom and uncle. It was hard to picture them her age or even as teens.

Anthony set the tape player at the end of the table and turned on a backup tape. "I'll take the lead on this one."

Bethany nodded, already tapping her toe in the grass and snapping her fingers to the beat of the music.

Stacia sat back and watched as her mom and uncle stood near the end of the table and sang song after song. A crowd gathered to listen—including the Best Friends, but the singers didn't seem to mind. Stacia noticed that Hannah and the others were listening intently, and she swelled with pride. She thought about joining them but felt too shy to move.

At the end of the fifth song Grandpa stood to his feet and snapped, "I'm going home. You can stay and make fools of yourselves if you want."

Anthony's face hardened. He caught his dad's

arm and said in a low, tight voice, "Do you always have to ruin everything?"

"Turn me loose, boy." Grandpa jerked free and strode to the car. He drove away without waiting for anyone.

Stacia squeezed Anthony's hand but couldn't think of anything to say.

Later they sat on the porch, and the adults talked while Stacia and the little girls listened. Tiffany fell asleep with her head on Stacia's lap.

Dad jumped up and carefully lifted Tiffany. "I'll lay her up on your bed, Sta. Want to come with me?"

Stacia hesitated, then nodded. This would be a good time to beg Dad to take her home with them. She followed him upstairs and pulled back the ugly plaid spread. Dad gently laid Tiffany down and pulled a light blanket over her. He smiled down at her with such love that jealousy ripped through Stacia. Dad really did love the little girls more than he did her!

Dad caught Stacia's hand and led her to the hallway. "I wanted a minute alone with you to see how you're doing. I know it can be hard to get along with your grandpa."

Stacia shrugged. She had so much she wanted to say to Dad, but she couldn't get a single word out.

12

Sunday

Stacia woke slowly, enjoying the sounds and smells and feel of her sisters sleeping with her. They'd spread a king-size blanket on the living room floor, and they all slept there, each with a warm blanket. Mom and Dad were sleeping in Stacia's room upstairs.

"Time to get up, girls." Stacia gently shook them. "I smell breakfast already."

Candace and Tiffany jumped right up, but Ariel snuggled down in her soft green cover.

Stacia laughed and snuggled down to Ariel. "Get up, sleepyhead. Grandma is making a good breakfast for you."

Ariel shook her head and moaned. She didn't like to eat breakfast any more than Stacia did.

"Help me fold the blankets." Stacia flipped a yellow blanket to Candace and Tiffany. They stood on each end of the blanket and started to fold it the best they could. Stacia lifted Ariel to the couch, then folded the other covers and stacked them with the pillows. Together they carried the blankets to the big linen closet near the downstairs bathroom.

Later the family gathered in the dining room for breakfast. The kitchen table was too small for all of them. Stacia liked having them all together. *This is the way it should be*, she thought. Anthony looked as if he hadn't slept much. Mom and Dad talked with Grandma and Grandpa while they ate eggs and toast and drank coffee.

Stacia finished breakfast as quickly as she could, then dressed in her blue flowered church dress. She helped the little girls get ready. Grandpa said it took only ten minutes to get to the church. At home it took them half an hour.

Anthony rode with Stacia and her family in the station wagon, and they followed Grandma and Grandpa in their car. Grandma had told them the church was different than their all-black church but that it was nice. She said usually they attended Sunday school, but it was too hard to get ready on time with so many in the house.

Inside the church Stacia sat between Anthony and Candace. The little girls had argued about who'd sit beside her, and Candace had won because she was the oldest of the three.

Stacia glanced quickly around. She counted five other African American families. She spotted

Chelsea and Hannah. They smiled and waved, and she lifted her hand in a tiny wave. She felt strange.

Anthony squeezed her hand and smiled.

She relaxed and enjoyed the singing, although it was different than at her church. She listened to the sermon and squirmed with guilt when she thought about Grandpa's garage window.

After church Hannah and Chelsea hurried over to Stacia before she could follow her family outdoors.

Chelsea smiled. "Hi, Stacia."

"We loved hearing the singing in the park yesterday," Hannah said.

"That was my mom and uncle."

"They're really good. I could've listened to them all day long!" Hannah stepped closer to Stacia. "Do you sing too?"

Stacia hesitated, then barely nodded. She thought of what Uncle Anthony had said and smiled. "I love to sing."

"We'd like to hear you," Chelsea said. "Could we come to your grandparents' house to listen sometime?"

"I'll ask them, but I think it would be all right."

"How about tomorrow?" Hannah asked.

"I'll ask." Stacia wanted to say she'd be back home tomorrow, but she knew she wouldn't be, no matter how badly she wanted to. "I'd better go. They're waiting in the car for me."

"What time will your family leave today?"

Stacia shrugged. Even the thought made her stomach sick. She couldn't speak over the lump in her throat.

"I might come over," Hannah said.

Stacia nodded.

"See you in school tomorrow." Chelsea smiled and walked away. Finally Hannah followed her.

Stacia hurried to the car. Warm wind blew against her. People hurried to their cars, some calling to others, some quiet. Stacia looked all around at the large parking lot. The station wagon was gone, and for a minute she panicked. Then she spotted Grandpa's car with Uncle Anthony driving it. She slipped in. "Hi. I'm sorry for keeping you waiting."

"No problem." Anthony turned up the radio as he drove out of the parking lot. "Listen . . . They're playing Leroy Drake."

Stacia listened, then frowned at Anthony. "He's okay, but you're better. How come you're not on tour as the artist instead of the road man?"

Anthony blew out his breath. "It takes more than a good voice to be the man behind the mike."

"Like what?"

"Courage."

"Courage? But you have lots of courage!"

"I hate to disappoint you, but I don't."

"Then get it!"

135

Anthony chuckled. "It's that easy, huh?"

"You know God answers prayer, right?"

Anthony nodded. He stopped at a stop sign and turned to Stacia. "I've had to compete with Pop's music all these years. I could never be as good as he was."

"No way! You're great!"

"We're family. You can't judge me fairly."

"You judged me. And we're family."

Anthony laughed and slapped the steering wheel. "You have a silver tongue, don't you?"

Stacia wrinkled her nose and giggled. "I know what I know."

Anthony pulled away from the stop sign and drove to The Ravines. "I ought to hire you as my manager."

"You can't. I'm going to be a singer . . . just like you said."

"Good for you. Don't let my fear stop you."

"I happen to know a Bible verse for you. It's 2 Timothy 1:7."

Anthony laughed as he pulled up behind his old brown van. "I know—I know—God didn't give me the spirit of fear. Keep it up, Stacia. I need all the encouragement I can get."

"And I need help too." She touched his hand on the steering wheel. "Will you please talk Mom and Dad into taking me home with them today?"

Anthony leaned over and kissed her cheek. "I can't, sweetcake. It's better for you to stay here."

Stacia jerked away from Anthony. Tears filled her eyes as she scrambled out of the car and ran to the house. She'd thought he'd understand, but he hadn't!

"What's wrong, Stacia?" Candace reached for Stacia's arm as she ran into the house after her.

Stacia brushed Candace's hand away. "Leave me alone!" Stacia raced upstairs to her room before she burst into wild tears. She closed and locked the door, then leaned heavily against it.

After a long time she pulled off her church dress and tugged on her jeans and white T-shirt with stars across the front.

Someone knocked, and she jumped.

"Stacia, dinner's on," Anthony said. "You ready?"

Stacia took a deep breath and slowly opened the door. "I can walk by myself."

"I know, but I want to walk with you. I'm sorry I couldn't do what you asked. I'm only thinking of what's best for you."

Without a word she hurried downstairs. She couldn't convince Anthony it was better for her to be home with her family, so why keep trying?

In the dining room Stacia sat between Ariel and Tiffany. Anthony sat between Stacia's parents.

Grandpa bowed his head and prayed over the

food before Stacia could close her eyes. She stared at him in surprise. He always had someone else bless the food. He looked up, and his eyes locked with hers. She flushed painfully and dropped her gaze to her hands locked in her lap.

Smells of roast beef, buttered carrots, and mashed potatoes filled the dining room. Stacia took a little of everything, even the tossed salad she didn't like very well. She forced herself to eat to give herself something to do and a reason to keep silent while the others chattered happily.

After dinner she helped with dishes because it was expected of her.

Mom hung up the dish towel and kissed Stacia's cheek. "I'm glad you're settling in so well."

Stacia shrugged. Why tell Mom the truth? It wouldn't do any good.

Mom rested her hands on Stacia's shoulders. "I had a great idea."

Stacia stiffened. "What?"

"Why don't you use your *King's Kids* money to pay for voice lessons?"

Stacia's heart dropped. She wanted voice lessons desperately, but she wanted to go home more. "I'm saving it for something else."

Mom frowned. "What?"

"I can't say."

"I hope it's not the dress you've been wanting."

Stacia shook her head. "Don't make me tell you, Mom. Please."

"All right, honey. Run and play with your sisters before we leave. We only have another hour."

"Another hour? Is that all?" Stacia flung herself into Mom's arms and held her fiercely.

An hour later Stacia stood beside her grandparents and uncle on the sidewalk and waved as her family drove away without her. Tears fell on the inside, but on the outside she looked as if it didn't bother her to have them leave.

Anthony rested a hand on Stacia's shoulder. "Want to sing together again before I have to take off?"

"No thanks." She stepped far enough away that his hand fell from her. "I have homework." She really did too. She just didn't know what it was. Maybe it was time she asked Hannah about the special assignment.

Stacia started for the house, then turned back. "I need to see Hannah Shigwam. I'll be back in about an hour."

"Hold it, sister!" Grandpa shook his finger at Stacia. "In this house you don't just tell us what your plans are—you get permission to do something."

Stacia bit back an angry remark. In a sticky sweet voice she said, "May I please visit Hannah Shigwam for an hour to do my homework?"

"Cut it out, Stacia King!" Anthony gripped her arms. "You should be happy that your folks love you enough to have you stay here to go to school."

His words sliced across her heart. Loved her? What did he know? She tensed but didn't pull away. She faced him squarely.

He sighed heavily and set her free. "I love you, Stacia Robedioux King. God is on your side, and you'll succeed as long as you keep your trust in Him."

Stacia ran down the sidewalk, her sneakers slapping against the concrete. It sounded like they were saying, "Stacia Robedioux King . . . Stacia Robedioux King . . . Stacia Robedioux King."

Hannah and Stacia

Hannah stared at Stacia as if she were a piece of bubble gum stuck on her shoe. They were sitting on Hannah's deck in back of the house. "How can you say you haven't done any part of the social studies assignment?"

Stacia hung her head. "You have every right to be angry. I'm sorry."

"You were supposed to think of the idea. You said you would!" Hannah heard the angry words echo inside her head. She stopped short. She mustn't act this way! She was supposed to forgive others. She was supposed to love like Jesus. She swallowed hard.

"I'm sorry, Stacia. I shouldn't have gotten angry."

Stacia looked up in shock. "But you had every right!"

"No. I'm supposed to be like Jesus. And so are you."

"I know. It's been so hard!"

"Because you're sad to be away from home."

"Sad, and mad too." Stacia hadn't admitted that to anyone but herself and Anthony. "I'm really really sorry for not doing my part of the assignment."

"I forgive you."

"I . . . don't even know what the assignment is."

"You don't?"

"I was daydreaming when the teacher talked about it, and then I was too mad to ask anyone. I wasn't even going to do it."

"I'm glad you changed your mind."

"Me too." Stacia grinned. "Will you tell me what I'm supposed to do?"

Hannah pulled her knees to her chin. "We have to write reports on things or people around us. It can be simple or complex."

Stacia fingered the Petoskey stone in her pocket. She'd showed it to her sisters before they left. Slowly Stacia held it out in the palm of her hand. "What about Petoskey stones? We could show several and tell about them."

Hannah laughed in delight. "Great idea! I like it. I hope nobody else thinks of it."

"We can ask Mrs. Prowess about the stones."

Stacia thought about her grandpa's collection. Her stomach knotted. Did she want to ask him? She cleared her throat. "My grandpa collects them too. We could ask him about them."

"I love it!" Hannah jumped to her feet. "I'll see if it's okay to do it right now."

"Right now?" Stacia fingered a strand of hair. "I don't know . . ."

"Why put it off? We can hand the report in early and have it out of the way."

"I guess so."

"I'll call Mrs. Prowess to see if we can stop by, and you call your grandpa to see if we can both talk to him and look at his collection."

"We'll just go see Grandpa without calling."

"Whatever you say."

Several minutes later the girls sat in Mrs. Prowess's kitchen with different sizes of Petoskey stones scattered on the table. Hannah had her notepad ready and her pencil poised over it.

Mrs. Prowess smiled proudly as she pushed stones around. "Did you know the Petoskey stone became Michigan's state stone in 1965?"

Stacia didn't know and really didn't care. She was only doing the assignment so neither she nor Hannah would fail the class.

Hannah quickly wrote the information in her notebook.

Mrs. Prowess held up a highly polished stone

and studied it in awe. "They're found along Lake Michigan near Petoskey, Michigan. The stones are composed of fossilized skeletons of colony coral that lived in the warm seas during the Devonian Period. Notice that they all have rounded edges."

Stacia had never heard of the Devonian Period, but she didn't want to say so. It sounded very boring to her.

Hannah picked up a small stone. "This looks like a piece of jewelry."

"My dear late husband was going to have it mounted in a bracelet for me but never did do it." Mrs. Prowess picked up another polished stone. "Look at the pattern of lines that branch out from the center of the six-sided shapes. It's truly a work of art."

"It is," Hannah whispered. She'd dropped her stone in her desk drawer, but when she got home she'd take it out and set it where everyone could see it. She hadn't realized how unique it was.

Stacia moved restlessly.

Hannah put the stone back on the table. "Stacia's Grandpa Smith has a collection of Petoskey stones too."

"How interesting. I'd like to see it sometime."

"Maybe he'll let me bring it over for you to look at." Stacia wanted to bite her tongue off for suggesting it. But it was too late. Even worse, she could see Mrs. Prowess liked the idea.

"How about tomorrow after school?"

"I'll ask Grandpa."

Mrs. Prowess smiled. "I'll be waiting for you."

Stacia nodded.

Outdoors Hannah stopped Stacia on the sidewalk. "Mrs. Prowess is a very lonely person. You will keep your word, won't you?"

Her eyes wide, Stacia jumped back a step. "Why would you think I wouldn't?"

"Look what you did to me."

"I know, and I'm sorry."

"And you can't get over being mad at your parents."

Stacia lifted her chin. "So?"

"So you might get so upset about still living here that you forget all about Mrs. Prowess."

Stacia thought about that and finally nodded. "You're right. But I won't forget. I wouldn't want to hurt Mrs. Prowess."

Hannah smiled. "Good. I believe you."

Stacia walked up the sidewalk with Hannah beside her. Seeing herself through Hannah's eyes shocked her. It was hard to think of herself lying, sassing, not doing homework, and—the real biggy—breaking the garage window because she was so angry. She glanced at Hannah. "Any news on the vandals?"

"There hasn't been any more trouble since your grandpa's and the Robbinses' windows were broken." Hannah pushed her hands into the pockets of her jeans and hunched her shoulders. "I'm ready to give up trying to find the guilty person or persons. I guess I'm not the detective I thought I was."

"Maybe you've been thinking of too many other things."

"Maybe." Hannah stopped.

Stacia did too. "What?"

"A terrible thought just popped into my head."

"What?" Stacia shivered, afraid of what it was.

"I've said all along that your garage window was broken with a rock instead of a club or bat or whatever."

"I've got to get home," Stacia said nervously.

"Did you break the window because you were upset about having to stay here?"

Stacia opened her mouth to say no, but she stopped herself. She did not lie! Finally she nodded.

"Oh my." Hannah bit her lip.

"I was going to tell, but I didn't have the nerve."

"But now you do. Right?"

Stacia squared her shoulders. "Right! I wasn't given the spirit of fear! I was given the spirit of love, of power, and a strong mind!"

Hannah laughed triumphantly. "And so was I!"

Stacia twisted a strand of hair around her finger. "Could we wait until another day to talk to Grandpa about the stones?"

"Sure. Why?"

"I want to tell him about the window."

Hannah smiled. "Good for you! Let me know how it comes out."

"I will." Stacia smiled slightly. "Hannah, thanks for being my friend even when I didn't want you to be."

Hannah nodded.

"And thanks for praying for me."

"Any time." Hannah silently thanked God for answering her prayers.

Later at home Stacia walked slowly down to the studio. She had to talk to Grandpa before she lost her courage. She carefully opened his door. He stood with his back to her, and he was singing. The words and the music sent chills over her. Anthony had been right. Grandpa could sing better than anyone she'd ever heard.

Just then he turned. His mouth was closed, but the music went on. It was a recording. He watched her as if waiting for a reaction.

Stacia silently entered the studio, closed the door, and just stood there until the music stopped. She brushed tears from her eyes. "You sing as beautiful as Uncle Anthony said you did."

Grandpa looked pleased, then scowled. "What are you doing down here?"

"I came to tell you something." The words sounded weak and trembling. "I . . . I . . . I broke the garage window."

Grandpa drew back a bit. "You? But why?"

She told him. "I'm really sorry. I wanted to tell you sooner, but I didn't have the nerve." She stopped talking, but he didn't say a word. "I'll pay you back. Just tell me how much."

He told her the amount. "You can pay a few dollars a month. Use the rest of the money for voice lessons."

She gasped in surprise. "I will."

"Sit down." He motioned to the director's chair.

Her legs trembling, she eased down into the chair.

"You have a great voice, but I don't want you wasting it like your uncle's doing."

"You don't understand him, Grandpa. He's too afraid to sing."

"Afraid! I never heard such garbage."

Stacia told Grandpa about her talk with Anthony and what she'd told him.

"You're a pretty smart girl." Grandpa paced the studio and finally perched on the edge of the desk, right where Anthony had. "You're old enough to hear my sad story."

Stacia locked her hands in her lap. Was she dreaming? Grandpa had never talked to her before—not really, and now he was going to tell her his story.

Grandpa rubbed a hand over his wiry hair. "I was making it as a recording artist, but I had to make a choice between being on the road or staying with my family. I wanted a family. So I chose staying home. I got a regular job. I blamed your grandma for losing out on my career. The anger ate away at me for what I had to give up."

"Why didn't you keep both your family and your music?"

"I didn't know how. And my dad said it wasn't right to try. He never liked my music. He said I should make an honest living—not waste my time singing and playing." Grandpa blinked tears from his eyes. "That's why I get so mad at Anthony. He's free to tour, free to make an album, but he won't do it. He'd rather follow along with a man who can't sing near as well as he can."

"I told you, Grandpa, he's afraid he can't be as good as you were. Or even as you are now."

"But he is as good!"

"You should tell him that."

Grandpa shrugged. "Why bother? He's as hard-headed as they come, and he won't listen."

"You should tell him anyway. And help him find the courage. You could do that, couldn't you?"

"Maybe so. Maybe so." Grandpa looked sharply at Stacia. "We got off-track here, girl. I want you to want a career so bad nothing will keep you from it. Find a way to sing no matter what it takes. Don't stop like I did. Don't go through the agony I went through." He lowered his voice. "I put my family through more pain than I can bear to think about."

"You can make up for it."

"How?" he snapped, his brows almost touching over his nose.

"I'll let you help me. And I bet Uncle Anthony would let you help him too." Stacia pushed herself up. "Let's go tell him now."

Grandpa shook his head. "He's gone."

Stacia felt as if she'd been kicked in the stomach. Anthony hadn't even told her good-bye! But could she blame him? She'd been so mean to him. "Do you know where he is?"

Grandpa pursed his lips, then nodded slightly.

"Then call him. Tell him we want to talk to him."

Grandpa shook his head. "I don't have the nerve."

"I told you about the garage window, and I didn't have the nerve. God didn't give you the spirit of fear . . ."

". . . but of love and power and a sound mind." Grandpa chuckled. "I used to say that verse a lot. But I let it kind of slip away. No longer!" He opened his studio door. "Let's go upstairs and call Anthony."

Stacia laughed and ran lightly upstairs with Grandpa close behind her.

14

Friends

With Grandma beside her, Stacia watched Grandpa and Anthony hug each other so long and hard she never thought they'd stop. She smiled at Grandpa, whose eyes were full of sparkling tears. After Grandpa's call, Anthony had come back home to talk to him, and Stacia felt sooo happy!

Finally Anthony turned to Stacia. "Thank you, Stacia Robedioux King! You helped work a miracle, and I'll never forget it."

"Someday I want us to sing together onstage. Then we'll remember this day and tell the audience all about it. It'll help them follow *their* dream."

"We'll make a date right now." Anthony chuckled, then kissed Stacia. "How about three years from now? Sooner if we're both ready."

"Done!" Grandpa wrapped an arm around Anthony and Stacia. "We heard that, didn't we, Parleen?"

"Clear as a bell." Grandma tapped Grandpa's shoulder. "And I want you to sing with them."

"Yes!" Anthony and Stacia cried together.

Grandpa didn't move for a long time. Finally he nodded. "I'll do it! The three of us will sing together."

Stacia laughed right out loud. And the next day in school she laughed again when she thought of it. She flushed and looked around quickly to make sure no one had heard. Students swarmed up and down the hall, slamming lockers, joking together, and heading for classes.

Just then Stacia spotted Roxie looking at Kathy and Roy. Tears slipped down Roxie's cheeks, and she quickly brushed them away as she turned to face her locker. Stacia silently prayed for Roxie. Suddenly Stacia stopped, her eyes wide. God really had worked a miracle inside her! It was as if she was so full of love she couldn't bring up any bad feelings—not even toward Roxie!

Smiling, Stacia hurried over to Roxie. "I'm sorry you're feeling bad," Stacia whispered. "Is there anything I can do?"

Roxie stared in surprise at Stacia. "I thought you hated me."

"I did, but I was wrong . . . wrong to be rude about the purple pig stuck in with your art. And I was wrong to snap at you every time I talked to you. I'm really sorry. Will you forgive me?"

"I can't believe what I'm hearing."

Just then Kathy and Roy walked past, talking and laughing.

Roxie froze. "I hate them both," she whispered fiercely.

Stacia shook her head. "Roxie, you're full of love—God's love. Let it shine through."

Roxie's mouth dropped open. "What happened to you?"

Stacia's face and neck burned. She deserved that. "I asked Jesus to forgive me for being such a brat, and He did. I remembered the Scripture that says God gave me a spirit of love, of power, and a sound mind."

Roxie scowled. "That's Kathy's favorite verse."

"It is?" Stacia turned and followed Roxie's gaze. Kathy and Roy were talking together outside the classroom door.

Roxie knotted her fists. "Just look at her! She's flirting with Roy now, but later she'll be all over Ty."

"You and Kathy should talk and settle your fight."

Chelsea and Hannah walked up in time to hear Stacia. "We both agree," Hannah said.

Chelsea nodded. "We're friends, Roxie. . . . best friends. We can't let anything keep us apart. Not even boys." Chelsea giggled. "Or an Oklahoma accent."

Roxie flushed. "Sorry about that."

"I already forgave you." Giggling, Chelsea flipped back her long red hair. "That's how I am—forgive and forget."

Stacia watched the three of them together. She felt left out. She started to walk away, then stopped. They didn't mean to leave her out, and she wasn't going to have hurt feelings over it. She stepped closer to Hannah. They smiled at each other, and Stacia felt better.

"I heard this morning the police caught the vandal." Hannah spread her hands. "This time they beat me to it."

"Do we know the person?" Roxie asked.

"Luke McFadden from The Ravines. He's seventeen and was mad at his dad. I don't know what his punishment will be."

Stacia patted Hannah's arm. "You'll solve the next one."

Hannah squared her shoulders. "I'll sure try!"

"Let's take a vote right now," Chelsea said. "Stacia, you get to vote too."

"Thanks." Stacia felt warm all over—as if she belonged. She might as well try to belong since she knew she had to stay until her family moved. But she'd be praying for Mom and Dad to find the right house in the right neighborhood so she could go home as soon as possible. She'd ask the Best Friends to pray too.

"What are we voting on?" Hannah asked.

"On Roxie and Kathy. Lift your hand if you say Roxie and Kathy should talk and make up." Grinning at Roxie, Chelsea lifted her hand.

Roxie made a face.

Hannah and Stacia lifted their hands, then took Roxie's hands and lifted them.

"It's unanimous." Chelsea motioned to the girls. "Come on, let's get this taken care of before the bell rings."

Roxie hung back. "I can't."

"Sure, you can."

"We're with you."

"So is Jesus."

Roxie helplessly shook her head.

The three girls tugged on Roxie until she giggled and walked with them.

Kathy saw them coming, and her heart jerked strangely. They were coming right up to her! Should she run? Were they going to tell her how terrible she'd been lately?

"I see your friends want you," Roy said with a chuckle. "I'll talk to you later."

Kathy nodded. Maybe she should flee to the restroom and hide in a stall. But she didn't move.

Chelsea pushed Roxie right up to Kathy. "We brought you two together so you could make up. No more fights. No more anger."

"Stacia and I agree," Hannah said.

Stacia nodded.

Kathy and Roxie looked at each other, then away, then back again. "I'm sorry," they both said at once.

Both girls laughed.

Kathy bit her lip. "What about Roy?"

Roxie took a deep breath. "I like him, but I won't stop being friends with you because of him."

Kathy smiled. "Me neither. We can all be friends with him, right?"

They all agreed.

"What about Ty?" Roxie asked.

Kathy made a face. "You all were right about him. I was wrong to hang out with him. Last night I asked God to forgive me for disobeying Him by spending too much time with Ty."

"Good for you," Hannah said softly.

They talked a while longer. Stacia locked her fingers together. "Girls, I'd like you to come over to my place after school today—after I show Mrs. Prowess Grandpa's Petoskey stone collection. I want to sing to you." Had she really said that? What if they laughed in her face?

"Sure, we'll come," they all said at the same time, then giggled.

After school and after showing Mrs. Prowess Grandpa's Petoskey stones, Stacia stood in Grandpa's studio while the girls sat in front of her. She clicked on the music and the mike. "This is a song my uncle wrote."

The Best Friends looked at each other and smiled.

Music leaped from the tape player, and Stacia lifted the mike to her mouth and sang the words Anthony had written. The beautiful words from her heart filled the studio. She sang better than she'd ever sung before. After all, she was singing for the Best Friends.

Roxie's eyes filled with tears. She moved closer to Kathy as Stacia sang on.

You are invited to become a *Best Friends Member!*

In becoming a member you'll receive a club membership card with your name on the front and a list of the Best Friends and their favorite Bible verses on the back along with a space for your favorite Scripture. You'll also receive a colorful, 2-inch, specially-made I'M A BEST FRIEND button and a write-up about the author, Hilda Stahl, with her autograph. As a bonus you'll get an occasional newsletter about the upcoming BEST FRIENDS books.

All you need to do is mail your NAME, ADDRESS (printed neatly, please), AGE and $3.00 for postage and handling to:

BEST FRIENDS
P.O. Box 96
Freeport, MI 49325

WELCOME TO THE CLUB!

(Authorized by the author, Hilda Stahl)